# CALL OF THE UNTAMED

## CALL OF THE LYCAN

## MICHELLE M. PILLOW

MICHELLE M. PILLOW® - MICHELLEPILLOW.COM

Call of the Untamed (Call of the Lycan) © Copyright 2007 - 2018, Michelle M. Pillow

Second Print Edition July 2018

First Print Edition September 25, 2017

Second Electronic Printing April 2011

First Electronic Printing January 2007

Published by The Raven Books LLC

ISBN 978-1-62501-194-7

## ABOUT CALL OF THE UNTAMED

## PARANORMAL SHIFTER ROMANCE

Roark O'Connell is a werewolf on the prowl. For what, he's not always sure. His job within the clan keeps him moving around and boredom often sets in. It's boredom that causes him to make a bet with his brother James to hire an etiquette coach. Expecting an old schoolmarm type, he's blown away to discover the most beautiful woman he's ever laid eyes on. The prim and proper Natasha might be there to tame his untamed ways, but he's just the man to fulfill her wildest dreams.

CALL OF THE LYCAN SERIES

Call of the Sea
Call of the Untamed
Call of Temptation

MICHELLE'S BESTSELLING SERIES

QURILIXEN WORLD NOVELS

**Dragon Lords Series**
Barbarian Prince
Perfect Prince
Dark Prince
Warrior Prince
His Highness The Duke
The Stubborn Lord
The Reluctant Lord
The Impatient Lord
The Dragon's Queen

*Lords of the Var*® **Series**
The Savage King

The Playful Prince
The Bound Prince
The Rogue Prince
The Pirate Prince

❖

**Captured by a Dragon-Shifter Series**
Determined Prince
Rebellious Prince
Stranded with the Cajun
Hunted by the Dragon
Mischievous Prince
Headstrong Prince

❖

**Space Lords Series**
His Frost Maiden
His Fire Maiden
His Metal Maiden
His Earth Maiden
His Woodland Maiden

❖

To stay informed about when a new book in the series installments is released, sign up for updates:

michellepillow.com/author-updates

*To the fans, thank you for your constant support.*

ROARK O'CONNELL SCRATCHED HIS ASS, yawning as he bumped into one of the many boxes lining his hallway. With a growl, he kicked at the ones partially blocking his bedroom door, causing his toe to get stuck in a cardboard side. The top of the small stack tumbled to the ground. Grumbling, he jerked his foot free, then immediately sweeping it so the boxes were pushed out of his way. Thank goodness they were lightweight and not filled with books. That would have hurt.

The knock again sounded on his front door, reminding him why he was standing upright before noon. It was only his brother James, coming to make sure he got out of bed in time to meet their oldest brother, Ian, who was flying into town with his new wife, Ceana. James was staying at a local hotel. As was his duty as a brother, Roark had offered to let James stay with him, but he'd declined. The last time they'd bunked together the two of them had gotten into a fistfight that would have ended in a funeral had they been humans. It wasn't the first time, and being that they were from a clan of natural-born lycans and were known to have high aggression levels, it wouldn't be the last. Besides, sparring was fun and they could instantly heal any of their own wounds.

*I'm coming!* he yelled, opening up the telepathic link he had with his brother. The knock sounded again, a short little rap against his door. *I said I'm coming. Hold your fucking horses.*

Leaning against the wall, he rubbed his temples, not really hurrying to answer it. The knock sounded again. Could James not hear him? Or was he purposefully being a jerk?

"You're early, dumbass," Roark growled to himself, knowing James' lycan senses would probably hear the insult. Though he was being grumpy, his brother could hardly take offense at his words.

James was eager to meet with his two brothers before he had to take off on a hunt. His target, Meghan, was a rogue lycan who had betrayed the clan when Ian didn't choose her as a bride. He instead picked Ceana. No doubt, that was what James wanted to consult with them about before going, since their father had appointed him to take the lead on the situation.

Ian's bride had been under a spell, which turned her into a mermaid. Ceana was a sweet woman, a little naïve for his taste, but she was perfect for Ian who had the patience to explain things like how to use a toilet and what stoplights were for. The newlyweds had been house shopping across the country. Roark personally thought it was an excuse for her to see everything she'd missed while in the water.

*You shouldn't have brought beer over last night, if you wanted me up this morning,* Roark said to him. *Ian and his bride will wait. It's not like we don't have an eternity to spend with them.*

Since becoming free of the centuries-old curse that an evil sea witch had cast upon her, Ceana had developed a fear of the sea. The woman knew more about the ocean than any other human, and she was deathly afraid of it. The O'Connells couldn't blame her for not wanting to step back into the sea. Though even she would admit the fear was unfounded since Ian's love broke the curse and the sea witch was dead—killed by her own arrogance. Being a lycan-mated human she had Ian's long life and health, not to mention the protection of the lycan clan.

Now Ian was bringing her into his area, looking for homes. Roark had moved to Kansas some time ago, and like he did every time he moved, he sent his brothers pictures of the area. Ceana had taken a liking to the landscape. Roark didn't care if they moved nearby, he hardly stayed put long enough to unpack—which was obvious by all the boxes. With modern transportation, it was no longer necessary for the clan to live close together. It wasn't like the old days when they'd have to be able to reach each other on foot in a single night, or be close enough to use telepathy. Just like with speech, the farther apart two lycans were, the harder it was to hear each other's thoughts—though telepathy did reach a lot farther than sound.

Now there were airplanes and cellular phones. In many ways, it had been a blessing. Roark loved his family, but no one could spend an eternity with the same people day after day—well, except if it was a mate. Their father, the king of the lycan clan, had even taken to using webcams for the clan meetings. Technically, Ian was next in line, then James and finally Roark. But, since they were immortal, pending some murderous rampage, it was unlikely that he'd ever rule. Roark was fine with that. He hunted for the clan, just like James, bringing justice to rogue wolves.

Stopping in confusion, Roark looked around. No, he wasn't in Kansas anymore. He'd moved from Kansas to somewhere else. Or did he just move to Kansas? Or did he move from one place in Kansas to another place in Kansas? It was too early and he was too hung-over to think about it. Maybe his family was right, maybe he needed to settle in one place and lay down some roots. Living out of boxes wasn't fun. It was just that he'd never found a reason to stay in any one place too long.

"Shit," he mumbled staring at a box that probably hadn't been unpacked in the last five moves. Blinking and yawning, he tried to kick-start his tired mind. The knock sounded again and he trudged forward. Pulling open the door, he closed his eyes briefly to the bright light of the day and grumbled, "I said I was coming, cocksucker. Now tell me, where the hell did I move to this time? I can't even remember for sure where I am."

"Oh my goodness!"

Roark stiffened in surprise. That didn't sound like James. Suddenly, he realized that James hadn't been answering back as he swore at him through the telepathic link. They must have drunk a lot more than he'd thought the night before. It was odd that he would be this out of it.

Roark focused his eyes on the beauty before him. It sure as hell didn't look like James either. Biting his lip, he moaned without thought, "Damn, baby."

What a way to wake up!

A slender woman with red hair stared at him. She glanced to the side, as if looking at his house. Her hair was pulled high on her head in a bun. Slowly, as she once more turned to look at him, she reached for her sunglasses and pushed them to the top of her head. Roark noted her vibrant blue eyes before letting his gaze travel down. She wore a dress suit—the charcoal gray skirt and jacket over the white silk shirt made for a very formal ensemble—and high-heeled shoes. Her legs were long and he couldn't help but wonder if he was still dreaming. If so, he really didn't want to wake up from this one.

No, dreams don't include hangovers.

"Sir," the woman said, breathing heavily as if she just now found her voice. Her cheeks were flushed and she clearly didn't like the way he'd answered his door. Roark smiled. He could easily make that up to her.

"Mmm." He leaned against the doorframe, putting up his arm to brace his weight.

"Sir," she repeated. Roark's smile widened. Her gaze rounded in mortification as her eyes traveled down. "Ah... *Sir!*"

Roark followed her troubled gaze. Not only had he forgotten that he was naked, he was also obviously aroused from staring at her. Grinning, and completely unapologetic, he winked at the sexy woman. "Morning wood."

"Sir, it's one p.m."

"Really? Hmm, okay, it's afternoon wood."

"Ah." The woman wrinkled her nose. "I'll come back later at a more..."

His smile widened as he gave her a come-hither look. There was something about her that made him want to act the beast. Very rarely did humans have that effect on him. She must have been very special indeed to provoke his body by just the mere sight of her.

In fact, Roark never had such a strong gut reaction to a human. They were a frail people and lycans tended to avoid them as much as possible. An ancient race, the lycans were as old as the humans, growing with them from the very beginning of time, just like all supernatural races. The Church used to condemn the supernaturals as evil pagans, going so far as to hunt and kill them. Times were wilder in the early days, but so it was with all the races—mortal and supernatural. Just as humans no longer roamed the countryside pillaging and wielding swords, his people no longer wildly wielded tooth and fang. Now the lycans hid their existence from the humans. It wasn't difficult, as they were able to smell their mortality instantly on them.

"Appropriate time," she finished weakly. Roark blinked, instantly drawn out of his racing thoughts.

"Why? You're here now." Roark left the door open and turned to go back to his bedroom to find something to put on. He heard her breath catch in her throat as he purposefully flexed his ass as he walked away. "Make yourself at home. I'll just be a moment."

❧

COCKSUCKER? *Did he really call her a cocksucker?*

Natasha Abbey stared at the naked man as he walked away from her. She held her breath in dismay. Well, at least she was pretty sure it was dismay. Whoever heard of someone greeting a person at the door in nothing but their male pride?

Never, when she woke up that morning, did Natasha expect to be welcomed by a naked man answering his front door. He was so not what she was expecting and she'd momentarily been stunned to silence. But having secretly worked with her fair share of Hollywood bad boys and rock stars, she liked to think she was used to their shocking and odd behavior.

This was supposed to be a job, just like any other job, though it was clear she had her work cut out for her. Her first task was to observe silently, make notes and then evaluate what lessons she needed to implement. Answering the door naked pretty much fell into the category of all-over etiquette makeover.

But there was another reason for her stunned silence. Never had she imagined that she would see a naked man so built and so obviously proud of his body—not to mention the fact that his cock had lifted to a towering height as soon as he looked at her. Tight muscles rippled beneath his flesh, from his perfect thighs to his taut ass, to his sculpted back and arms. Long waist-length, dark brown hair flowed in perfect waves down his back.

*This is Roark O'Connell?*
*This is my new client?*
*Oh. My. Stars.*

Natasha's heart leapt in her chest, but the quickening wasn't love at first sight so much as fiery lust at first glance. That was good, because she wasn't necessarily looking for love. Other things came first. She had yet to figure out exactly what those other things were, but she was sure they were out there. Love had never really interested her. It seemed too clichéd, too straight out of some cheesy movie, too long a time for a woman with her extremely unique background to commit to one person. At least, that had been true up until seven years ago when she was cursed into her current form. She didn't know the full extent of what the farfadet elders had done to her, but she could only guess that with her new human form also came human mortality. When she cut herself now, she bled and didn't heal right away. She could catch colds, tired easily and had no powers whatsoever. Farfadets normally slipped through time with ease. All she could do was go forward at a human pace.

Leaning over, she grabbed her briefcase and slowly backed away from the opened door. She glanced up to the eave of the house, checking the address to make sure it was correct. To her horror, it was. She was at the right place.

Did she leave? Make a run from the sexy, crazy man? Or did she do her job like the professional she was? Natasha took a deep breath and lifted her chin. She was a professional. She would not let this man and his lack of manners upset her. No doubt he, out of all her other clients, was in desperate need of her services.

Still, there was that nagging feeling, a part of her old life that stirred within her at seeing him. Maybe it was the awakened desire she felt like never before. Since turning, she'd been alone. Human intimacy frightened her, as they often contributed more emotion to the act of intercourse than was actually due the situation. It's not like she could time slip away afterward if she didn't want to face the man or if he was bad in bed.

The second she'd seen Roark, her heartbeat accelerated and she felt helpless and weak. Natasha wasn't a weak person.

Stepping back to the door, she hesitated before going inside. She had to step around boxes to get to the living room. The house was nice. Who was she kidding? It was more than nice, it was fabulous. But why did a man who owned a mini-mansion have boxes everywhere? Did he just move in? The memo from her office listed this as a new address, which would explain things. A few of the boxes were ripped open and clothes were draped over them onto the floor.

*He's a slob! A gorgeous, rude slob.*

Natasha's apartment might have been small, but it was immaculate. Wrinkling her nose, she saw a half-opened pizza box stuffed with used paper towels on the coffee table before an expensive flat-screen television. DVD movie boxes were strewn over the coffee table and floor, stacked on the low cabinet under the flat screen. More movies were on two bookcases along the walls. She frowned. Did the man do anything besides watch movies? Without thinking, she set down her briefcase and grabbed the box before going to find a trash can. Heels made it hard to walk through the maze of boxes and she was forced to put her arms out to the side for balance.

"Mmm, *a thaisce*, you've come to find me," Roark said, his voice low, and suddenly thick with a soft burr of an accent. By the way he said *"a thaisce"* it was clearly an endearment. "I wouldn't have put pants on if I knew you were going to change your mind and follow me back."

Natasha gasped, shivering as Roark slipped a hand along her waist from behind. The warmth of his palm spread out over her, causing her to loosen her grip on the box. It crashed to the floor. The instant she let go of the trash, Roark swung her around and lifted her off the ground. His body pressed into hers, sending a magnificent shock down her. Grabbing her hand and lifting it to the side, he began to hum, dancing to his own song as he artfully moved her down the hall, weaving around the boxes, toward the living room. Her feet dangled off the floor. The arm around her waist held her tight to his naked chest. She was thankful that he said he wore pants, but as she felt the still very aroused press of his cock to her hip, she stiffened.

"Ah, Mr. O'Connell, please," Natasha said, trying weakly to hit him with the hand that was trapped to his chest. A very large, wicked part of her wanted to let him continue. Prudence took over as she suppressed the base urge. "Put me down this instant."

He did so, abruptly spinning her away from him in a graceful move—at least on his part. Natasha stumbled only to catch herself. Making a weak noise, she smoothed down her skirt and straightened her jacket, before patting down her hair. When she finally looked up at Roark, she stiffened. He'd gotten dressed, all right—in a pair of skin-tight, hip-riding black leather pants. A trail of hair led down his stomach to beneath the leather. By the tightness of the pants, it was pretty clear by the lack of lines that he wasn't wearing underwear.

*The man looks like a rock star. Wonderful,* she thought sarcastically. *I've been hired by a supermodel rock star with a libido hot enough to do any man proud and the cock to back it up.*

Natasha took several deep breaths. Roark's long wild hair spilled over his chest and shoulders. It matched the untamed light in his dark eyes. Taking a second look, she shivered. His eyes looked lighter than before, almost like a yellow-brown hazel. She'd been sure they were darker.

*I've dealt with rock stars before. I just have to remain professional. When he sees he can't shock me, he'll stop and behave.*

"So," Roark said, teasingly. "Are you a maid for hire? Or do you just start cleaning every house you walk into?"

She blinked, slightly confused by the joke as she looked down at her business suit. Then, remembering that she'd indeed picked up the pizza box when she'd first walked in, she gave a halfhearted laugh.

It hit her that she hadn't introduced herself. From being called a cocksucker, to seeing a gorgeous naked man open the door, to being held tight in the sexiest embrace she'd ever been a part of, she'd lost her wits.

Clearing her throat, she held out her hand. "Mr. O'Connell, I'm Natasha Abbey."

He didn't move, looking completely blank.

"You hired me," she said carefully.

Again, he didn't move.

"We have an appointment to go over your plans. I just flew in from New York to be here. Your assistant confirmed just last week and gave me the new address. We would've called you, but you didn't have a number on file."

Still nothing.

"You called my office requesting my services. I admit it's been several months since you scheduled, but you did pay in advance." She frowned. What was wrong with this guy? "You are Mr. Roark O'Connell, are you not?"

"Just Roark, love," he said. "Mr. O'Connell is my father's name."

"Charming," she muttered, not really meaning it. The last words had been said with a distinctly Irish accent and she had no doubt he was parodying one of his movies. No matter the race, she found men tended to do that, quoting movies or plays as if it were a real talent. "You don't remember hiring me for the week?"

"Um, are you a maid?" he asked, glancing to where she'd dropped the pizza box. "You don't look like a maid and I don't know any that fly across country to clean, but I can't for the life of me think of anything else."

"No, I'm not a maid," she answered.

He shrugged. "Well, then, tell me what it is I hired you for and I'll tell you if I remember doing it."

"I'm an etiquette and image consultant. Several months ago you called my offices and told my secretary that you enjoyed my article on table etiquette and wished for me to move in with you to teach you... Does any of this sound familiar, sir?"

He grinned, running his eyes down her body. "You're going to live with me? Mmm, I just might have to renovate all the guest bedrooms. But the master bedroom will be free until all that's done."

Natasha ignored the innuendo of her sleeping with him in his bed for a week. She'd dealt with his rich and famous type before and their supermodel, anorexic girlfriends. She could handle one man. Since she didn't listen to rock music, it was no surprise that she'd never heard of him before. But that wasn't the first time she hadn't heard of some famous client. She'd once spent a whole week with a baseball player before she realized just how famous he was. The men in her office building had been in total awe. But the way her company kept her busy going from job to job, it wasn't like she stopped to look every client up on the Internet. And, being a farfadet, fame didn't really faze her as it did most mortals. In fact, she didn't care. It made the secrecy part of her work easy—as the majority of her clients didn't want their lessons going public. Before a job, sometimes all she got was a name, a location, and a basic request of for services. Fame didn't change the way she handled herself professionally and it was better for her if she didn't have any media-induced, preconceived notions in her head. She liked the first impression of a client to be genuine. It helped her to do her job. If she had their latest scandal in the back of her mind, then it was too easy to focus on that one issue and not the whole picture.

Roark grinned, a completely incorrigible look. "I hope you don't mind sharing a bed. If I steal covers, you can cuddle next to me for warmth."

It seemed he had no problem getting to the point, or keeping with the point until he got a reaction. Maybe it was her lack of reaction to his come-ons that was baffling him and causing him to keep them up. Taking a long, calming breath, she did her best to sound businesslike. "No, we explained that wouldn't be appropriate. I'll be staying at the local hotel for the duration of the training."

"Ah, so you won't be staying here?" He hummed softly, looking disappointed.

The man was persistent, she'd give him that. No doubt he was about to sign some record deal or something and his agent wanted him to learn some manners. Glancing around his home, she could see why his agent would be concerned. The man needed organization and focus. A home said a lot about a person. She took a deep breath. No doubt this would be an easy one—chewing with the mouth closed, interview etiquette and training, not urinating in public, some personal grooming lessons...

*Not that he looks all that poorly groomed.*

Natasha shivered. Too bad she couldn't work spells anymore, otherwise she'd put a block on herself when it came to him. There was a base, natural, hard attraction to him that she felt all the way to her bones. Almost as if her world would end if she didn't submit to the desire to have sex with him. But that was stupid. She was just in need of a man and he was the first one she'd been attracted to in ages.

"Why don't we begin?" Natasha crossed the

room to her briefcase and set it on the coffee table where the pizza box had been. It might be hard, but she would keep their interaction strictly professional. Opening it, she took out her favorite designer pen and a fresh notepad. Perching her butt on the end of his couch, she looked expectantly at him. "What exactly is your primary goal?"

Roark tilted his head to the side, his lip curling slightly as if in deep thought. "Mmm, yeah, I remember now. I was drunk and my brother James dared me to call you. That's right." He slowly walked to an overstuffed chair and sat across from her. Grabbing a pack of cigarettes off a side table, he lit up. Smoke curled around him and he motioned at her with the cigarette. "We have a bet going on whether or not you will quit before a week is out. Damn, I forgot we'd made that appointment. No wonder James came over last night with pizza and beer. I should've known something was up. He wants to win the bet."

"A bet?" she repeated. Slowly, she closed her pen and put the notepad back into her briefcase. "James is the name of your brother? He wasn't your assistant?"

"Ah, so that's who called to give you my address. I should've known something was up when he offered to buy the good beer." Roark gave a small laugh.

"So you're not an aspiring musician?

"Is that what James said?" He chuckled. "No, no, I'm not. Though I've been told I can make women sing."

*Charming*, she thought sarcastically.

"What do you do?" she asked.

"Not much of anything really."

"Mr. O'Connell—"

"Roark."

"Mr. O'Connell," she coughed, waving her hand as smoke drifted in her face. "Do you mind? If you haven't heard, smoking can kill you and whereas I don't know if suicide is your intention, I'd like to live a while longer."

Especially since her human lungs were prone to mortal diseases, she had to be careful now. The threat of death tended to make a girl cautious.

She took a deep breath, trying to calm herself. There was no need to get short-tempered and her last comment had been a little mean. It was just the man baffled her and made it hard to concentrate.

"I heard that, but then I'm not human," he said, winking audaciously. Still, he put the cigarette out.

"It won't do a damned thing to me. I plan on living forever or die trying."

"Ah." Natasha wondered if the man thought his joke was funny. If the man only knew the true meaning of not being human. "Mr. O'Connell, I take my job very seriously—"

"I see that. You seem to take everything seriously."

"*And*," she stressed, irritated by the interruption, "I don't appreciate being called all the way to Kansas on a drunken bet because you and your brother have trust funds and too much time on your hands."

"Huh, so I am still in Kansas." He shook his head before rubbing the bridge of his nose as if in deep thought.

Natasha closed the briefcase and stood. "It was a pleasure to meet you, Mr. O'Connell. I can show myself out."

"You call that a pleasure?" he chuckled, pushing up from the chair to follow her. "*A thaisce*, if that is what passes in your book as a pleasure, please allow me to show you more."

"Sexual harassment, Mr. O'Connell," she quipped.

"Pneumonoultramicroscopicsilicovolcanokoniosis." Roark smiled.

"Excuse me?"

"Pneumonoultramicroscopicsilicovolcanokoniosis," he repeated. "The lung disease caused by inhaling very fine silica particles."

"What?" Was this man crazy? Was she crazy for standing here listening?

"Pneumonoultramicroscopicsilicovolcanokoniosis." His grin widened. "You were using big words, I thought I would too. It's the longest word in the English language at forty-five letters."

"What?" she repeated, trying to follow his sudden turn of the conversation.

"You said harassment."

"What?"

"Oh, there's also hepaticocholangiocholecystenterostomies, the surgical connections between the gall bladder and the hepatic duct, coming in at thirty-nine letters."

"But—"

"Now, I know what you're going to say—"

"Ah, but—"

"What                                        about 'Supercalifragilisticexpialidocious'?"

"No—"

"That was just a song title made up in the late nineteen-forties, early nineteen-fifties by Parker and

Young and only has, ah, thirty-five, no sorry, thirty-four letters. Though if you are going non-medical words, I suppose that could be it. Huh, I'll have to check on that and get back to you."

Natasha shook her head, completely turned around by his illogical train of thought. "Mr. O'Connell! What are you going on about?"

As if it was the most normal thing in the world, he looked at her as if she was the crazy one. "Words."

"What? Are you some sort of word trivia nut?"

"Damn, *a thaisce*, you are wonderfully disorientated when you're not acting proper." He winked.

"You are just doing this to test me?" She gasped. "To see if you can confuse me?"

"And to get you to stay," he admitted, grinning like a little boy who'd gotten his way. Why did the insufferable man have to look so sexy when he smiled? And why did his eyes gleam with such obvious sexual invitation?

"I'm not staying," Natasha informed him. "And I don't appreciate you trying to manipulate me or confuse me or whatever it is you're trying to do."

"Oh, good idea. I don't have anything to eat here. Let's go out. I'll show you the town."

"What? No. No. Please, no. If I go now I can surely get on a flight back to New York tonight." Did this man even know where food was? He didn't know what state he was in. She trembled, part of her screaming that she needed to take this excuse and go. If she was around him much longer, the natural urgings of her body would surely tempt her into doing something stupid.

"*A thaisce*, you took my money. The least you could do it give me the lessons I paid for."

With disdain dripping from her tone, she said dryly, "I'll refund it."

"Your secretary made me sign a contract. That binds you as well as me. I don't want a refund. And you don't want to be sued for discrimination, do you? Ah, discrimination. Not the longest word, but a good one, don't you think?"

Natasha could feel the blood draining out of her face. Some insane part of her wanted to stay, was glad that he was tricking her. That part of herself scared her.

"Fine," she quipped. "But we need to go over the ground rules."

"So I get the two weeks I paid for?" he asked.

"You only paid for a week in advance. I'm sorry, but I'm booked after that."

"Can't blame a guy for trying. Just let me grab a

shirt, that is, unless you'd like to keep staring at my chest? I have no problem taking you out like this."

Natasha pried her eyes up. Was she staring at him?

Oh, goodness! She was.

"Chemistry," he said softly. "Another good word."

She couldn't answer.

"I'll be right back. Don't run away, precious," Roark turned, heading down the hall. When he was gone, she hurried out of the house, taking several deep breaths as she searched for her rental car keys.

"Oh, Natasha," she whispered, "what have you gotten yourself into now?"

ROARK GRINNED, looking into his motorcycle's rearview mirror to see Natasha still following behind him. He had forgotten about hiring her until she said something. The woman was booked solid and they'd made the bet over six months ago. From her article, both brothers expected her to be an old schoolmarm type. James had thought it hilarious to force an old, proper woman on his wild younger brother.

Natasha Abbey was definitely no old schoolmarm.

Roark's smile only widened. He could tell he frustrated her, but he couldn't seem to stop himself from pushing her buttons. Wiggling in his seat, he tried to adjust himself without being obvious. The pants were sexy and he knew they looked good on him, but they weren't practical for riding his old motorcycle and they did tend to get a little too snug whenever he became aroused—which he had been since seeing the redheaded bombshell on his front step.

He'd offered to give her a ride on his bike and had to admit he was relieved when she said no, insisting they take separate vehicles. If her proper little body had pressed against his back for the short duration of the trip, he'd surely shift into full lycan and take her alongside the interstate. Normally, simple sexual arousal wasn't enough to bring on the change, but what he was feeling went beyond that into hot, fiery passion. Whenever a lycan was impassioned—whether it was lust, anger or any other variety of strong emotions—it became hard to control the inner beast.

His father would *love* that. The man would undoubtedly have him imprisoned for causing such a public display like shifting in public to take a human female. And his older brother, Ian, the future king, would undoubtedly help to trap him. Lycan prisons weren't like human prisons. They were treated like the dogs they could be. Roark knew. He'd been caught by Queen Victoria's guards screwing one of her chambermaids in half shift. Luckily, they didn't have surveillance cameras back then and no one believed the guards when they said he'd been half wolf.

*Poor bastards.*

The guards had been relieved of duty because of the incident. Roark had made it right, though they never would've known it. He wished he could've been so lucky. The human jail would've been better than being tried by his own kind for drawing attention to them. It had been a close call, but he still spent six months behind bars for it.

Nowadays, even Roark admitted they needed to be more discreet. One mistake and they'd find themselves on every newscast worldwide. The clans wouldn't be too happy about that. Only a few humans knew of their existence. It wasn't because the lycans were ashamed, but because humans were simply not ready to know about them. They'd become enamored with science and logic. There was no room for magic in the civilized world anymore.

Taking a left, he kept his speed down. Natasha followed the speed limit to the number. It was no surprise. The woman clearly lacked any fun in her life. It was almost as if she was frightened. Maybe it was his calling to help her break out of her shell. It was clear by her scent that she was interested in him, otherwise he'd never have bothered her with persistent come-on lines. He wasn't a complete cad.

Glancing into his rearview mirror, he suddenly imagined having the prim and proper Natasha bent over, her suit skirt hiked up around her hips as he pumped his stiff cock into her sweet-smelling body.

*Okay, I am a cad. I am. But, lycans help me, she's just too sexy to be let out without a leash.*

That thought only led to more. How he'd like to tie Natasha up and slowly torture her until she orgasmed so hard she would never leave his bed. Roark had always had a thing for leather and light bondage. Though he didn't get into domination in the true sense of the word. He liked his woman to express herself freely without his commands and he did sometimes like being dominated.

*I bet you'd know how to dominate me, wouldn't you, Natasha? You'd like telling me what to do, wouldn't you?*

Roark began to sweat. His cock hurt so badly it throbbed beneath his tight pants. It had been a long time since the mere thought of fucking a woman made him this hot. Claws threatened to grow from his fingertips and he was glad his sunglasses would hide the liquid amber of his eyes. Would she protest the beast in him? Would she kneel before him in such a state and suck him dry?

Roark's heart pounded. This was getting out of his control. The wolf in him was sending images of its own through his head—images of Natasha taking his shifted cock in her mouth, of Natasha bent over on all fours as he rammed himself home in her sweet, wet sex and her tight, perfect ass.

Letting the beast out to play wasn't good. Human women couldn't handle the size of the wolf. He'd shred her to bits if he were to try.

*I need to get laid, and soon. Otherwise, I won't be able to hold back.*

Roark again glanced in the mirror, seeing a glimpse of sunlight on Natasha's red hair. Swallowing over the lump in his throat, he blinked and tried to determine where he was going. They were supposed to be getting lunch. Seeing that he'd automatically driven to a little diner he'd been at the day before, he turned into the parking lot. He could well afford to take her to the most expensive restaurants, but he had a feeling his dangerous, "bad boy" side turned her on. In the very least, she'd seemed to enjoy staring at him in tight leather pants.

Roark shut off his engine and swung his leg over his bike. The motorcycle was his favorite vehicle and he had to admit most women found it attractive. Turning to the one woman he really wanted to impress, he reached to open the car door for Natasha. He purposefully stood too close as she stepped out.

"Thank you, Mr. O'Connell," she nodded in approval, "your manners aren't a complete loss, I see."

When she stood from the car, he didn't move back to give her space. The scent of her filled his nostrils. Her breath caught and she made a weak move as if to push past him. Roark put his hand on the top of the car to stop her.

"You know, Ms. Abbey, you are one hell of a sexy woman and you smell really nice."

"Excuse me?"

"I said," Roark leaned closer to her, "that you are a very sexy woman, *a thaisce*, and I would be more than willing to service you in any way you desire."

Natasha paled. Her eyes darted to his lips. He detected the instant gush of cream between her thighs. The smell of it tortured him.

"Are...? Are you serious?" she whispered.

"Mmm, just grab my cock if you don't believe me. I can't seem to keep it down around you." He leaned closer, not knowing what was coming over him. She smelled so good and he loved that she wasn't protesting his boldness. "I can't ever remember having such a strong reaction to a woman. Can't you feel it? It's like you've invaded my blood and heated my body to the point of explosion. All I can think about is fucking you."

"This isn't... Ah. Um. Well, you..." Her breathing deepened. "You shouldn't be saying these things."

"It's not," Roark grinned, leaning a little closer to her perfect mouth, "proper etiquette?"

"No, it's not," she whispered, not backing away. If anything, she swayed forward ever so slightly, as if closing the distance between their mouths. Her eyes glazed as she stared at his lips. "Please, I'm here to do a job. I'm supposed to be teaching you not to do these sorts of things."

"You mentioned wanting to lay some ground rules at the house." Roark waited as she nodded in agreement. "I'd be happy to lay some for you, just to see how you like them. First, give me permission to show you pleasure like you've never had before and I promise to be as discreet as you want. Your office will never find out. Hell, I won't tell a soul. At all. Second, I'll let you teach me manners and I promise to be a good student, if you let me teach you how to let go a little and have some fun."

Her breath hitched, "Mr. O'Connell—"

"Third, you must call me Roark." Grinning wickedly, he added, "Unless you're wanting to role play in which case I'm game."

"Roark, please. I'll admit there's some attraction between us and it may even be strong, but—"

He could see the denial in her eyes and he hastened to try and convince her to give in to him and the arousal he detected coming from her. "Just hear what I am offering you, Natasha, think about it. You can use me for whatever wild fantasies, for whatever tawdry, dirty, depraved little sex acts you've denied yourself and I'll give in to your whims completely. Come on, *a thaisce*. Isn't there a part of you wanting to give in to me? A wild side you've kept on a leash? It's only a week. You're in Kansas City, Kansas. No one here knows you. There will be no commitments afterward. What do you say?"

"I'm surprised you know what city you're in," she said.

"I saw a sign when we were driving and that's not an answer." Roark didn't like thinking that there would be no commitment afterward, but really it was for the best. She was human, after all, and lycans didn't mate to humans. Sure, lycans had been known to take humans to their beds. They dated them and some even spent lifetimes with them. But they never mated with them, not for all eternity. Only other immortal supernaturals were suitable lifemates. Too many lycans had seen their loved ones die as they tried to turn them. It was a painful memory that would be carried into eternity. For, if not murdered, the lycan would live forever.

Occasionally, lines would be blurred and mortals would be turned. Lycans were lusty creatures after all, craving both blood and sex. Circumstances had to be right—the bloodline perfect and the moon full—for the bite to take effect. Even so, it was against the law to turn mortals. A lycan could attack fifty humans and only possibly turn one. So if a human was turned, the odds were that lycan had attacked many—unless it was a special circumstance. Even then, it didn't guarantee they'd make it through the horrifically painful process.

It was why his kind didn't mate with humans. Sex with them, sure. Mating, no.

Roark frowned. Why was he suddenly thinking of turning humans into lycans? Though he wouldn't mind inviting this one in to help him tame his inner beast, but to have thoughts of eternity?

"What do you say?" he asked again. Every nerve in him seemed to stretch toward her. He needed her desperately, wanted her terribly.

"I say." She took several deep breaths. "I say that we came here for lunch."

In physical pain at her refusal to agree to his plan, he took a step back. Her eyes darted down to his hip, to where his arousal pressed against tight leather. She made a weak noise and turned her eyes away.

*You are something, aren't you, Ms. Abbey? I only hope you don't have too much willpower when it comes to denying your body and mine.*

❧

NATASHA COULDN'T BELIEVE ROARK. The audacity! The sheer boldness! The...all too incredibly tempting arrangement!

*I can't. No. It's not right. I can't take him up on his offer.*

*But he does have a good point,* her inner voice argued. *No one will look for you here. No one will know about it. How long has it been anyway since a man was between those thighs of yours? Are you sure they're not rusted shut?*

Natasha grimaced. It had been awhile since she had sex, unless a vibrator counted, in which case she'd burnt out the last three. Being from her "special, unmentionable" heritage made her sexually active by nature, even if she was cursed into the body of a human. But for years she denied her past, trying to blend in, trying to learn the mortal ways.

*Don't think of it. You are human. If you think of the old ways, they'll come for you. You are human. You are human. Be the human.*

*Ugh.*

"The supernatural do not exist," she whispered, wishing there was a way to make herself truly believe it.

"Pardon me?" Roark pulled open the door to the diner, holding it for her so she could go inside. When she stepped past him, she felt the faintest brush on her ass. She glanced back. The man looked too inno-cent to be believed.

"I didn't say anything," she lied.

"Hmm, I must be hearing things. Either that, or I was hoping you were finally willing to answer me about my offer."

"You've hired me to do a job, Mr. O'Connell, and I intend to do that job." She nodded smartly at him and stepped into the diner. It had booth seats and waitresses dressed in old fifties outfits. Classic rock played over the intercom and small jukeboxes were in the booths on each table.

"Two please," Roark said to the hostess, offering his arm to Natasha.

"Roark, you devil. Welcome back, sweetie pie."

Natasha arched a brow. "Come here often?"

"No, just yesterday." He looked uncomfortable.

"The girls can't stop talking about how good you dance," the hostess said. "Where did you learn to move like that? Tell the truth, now. Dance lessons?"

"Yeah," he laughed. "Tell the ladies I had a lot of fun with them too."

"Dance?" Natasha asked.

"It's nothing," he said under his breath. "We were just bored. The place was dead and they do have great music."

"Bored?" the lady laughed. Then, with a pointed look at Natasha, she said, "You didn't know you were on a date with a stripper, did you?"

Natasha gasped, looking at Roark. He grinned, shrugged and sat down. "Like I said, we were bored."

The woman seated them at a table in the back. The place was nearly empty, except for a few families who dined in the other side of the restaurant. The high-pitched whine of a young child drifted over the diner, only to be followed by the shushing of the kid's parents. Seeing an ashtray on the table, she began to lift her hand to have the woman seat them in non-smoking.

Roark grabbed her hand and held it in his. Slowly running his fingers over her wrist, he said, "I won't light up. In fact, I'm giving the habit up."

"Really?" Was it her, or was his skin really hot? She felt the spark of his touch all the way up her arm. It was as if she could feel it against her breasts as her nipples hardened into treacherous little peaks. Thank goodness she was wearing the suit jacket—even if it did feel a little hot.

"Mmm, you like when I touch you, don't you?" He took a deep breath, as he lifted her hand to his mouth. Weak, and frankly too stunned to pull back, she let him. Roark lightly flicked his tongue over her wrist and palm before kissing it with an open mouth. He groaned, doing it again and again, as he ran his mouth along her forearm. "I'm suddenly not hungry. How about we take off and go back to my place?"

Natasha pulled her hand from him in mid-kiss. "I'm famished."

Roark grumbled, but didn't say anything she could understand as the waitress came to take their order. Not surprising, he got a steak with numerous unhealthy side dishes. Natasha ordered a salad and water.

He started flipping through the selection of songs on the miniature jukebox on their table. The unit was nailed to the wall and had an impressive number of song choices. Within moments, classic Fifties rock blared overhead. It had a fast upbeat tempo and the voice that belted along with the music was as smooth as silk.

"You have a beautiful mouth," he said. "And a nice voice."

Had she started singing under her breath again? It was a horrible habit. Ignoring the compliment, she said, "Well, let's start, shall we?"

"What? Here?" Roark glanced behind his back, a small smile on his face when he again looked at her. "You want to do it in the restroom?"

*YES!*

"No, the etiquette lessons," Natasha told him emphatically. This was only the first afternoon. How was she going to resist him for a week? Especially when her body was already turned on by him? "We want to make sure you get your money's worth, don't we?"

"Not really," he grumbled.

Natasha ignored his griping. "Let's start with table manners, shall we? Dining etiquette is essential to making a good impression and speaks volumes about a person." Unrolling the silverware from the napkin, she placed it on the table in front of her, positioning the fork, knife and spoon in proper order. "Since we don't have a full service in front of us, this will have to do." She reached over, arranging his as well. "If this were a small luncheon napkin, you would unfold it completely. But, since it's a full-size dinner napkin, you only fold it into half like so. Now, it's customary for you to wait until your host or hostess unfolds their napkin first. You don't want to come off as too eager to dine."

Roark didn't move.

"Go on," she urged. "Pretend I'm the hostess. See, I've just unfolded my napkin and set it in my lap."

Slowly, a frown marring his brow, he did the same. She nodded in approval.

"The napkin is to stay on your lap at all times. If you get up and put the napkin on your plate, that will tell your server you are not coming back and that they may take your plate away. The meal is over when the host or hostess puts their napkin on the table to the right of their plate like so." Natasha placed her napkin on the table. "Now you try. Don't wad it up into a ball, but don't refold it either."

Roark didn't look pleased, but he followed her example.

The waitress came and delivered their drinks, placing them on the table. As he reached for his, Natasha took it away and set it to the right of his plate. "Glassware will always be placed here. It's important when drinking to put your glass down in the same place, as to maintain the visual integrity of the dining area."

The waitress snorted at her. Natasha scowled slightly in disapproval. Roark laughed, grabbing his glass and taking a drink of his soda.

"It's easy to remember where things in the place settings go. Liquids on the right," Natasha pointed to the right of her plate before motioning gracefully to the other side, "and solids on the left."

Roark leaned forward. "I'm sorry, love, but this is boring. I'd much rather talk about you."

"That very well may be, but manners are ways of showing other people that you respect them."

"Do they teach you to say things like that?" he asked.

"You pay me to say things like that. In fact, a lot of celebrities pay me to train their future wives and husbands in the art of etiquette. When people are public figures they are under constant watch. If a person is not born into the lifestyle, then one must learn the lifestyle."

"Ah, so if I pay you more, you'll let me eat in peace?" He winked to soften his words. "'Cause the way I see it, the more money you have, the more people will like you regardless of your table manners."

"Just be happy I don't make you sit through a lecture on the difference between the American way of cutting meat and the Continental way."

"Did you just make a joke?" he asked, appearing truly amazed. "Say it isn't so! Are you showing signs of loosening up?"

"Highly doubtful," she assured him. "Silverware usage is easy. Just start from the outside and work your way in."

"You know, I'm easy as well."

She couldn't help but laugh. Wryly, she shook her head. "So you keep telling me."

"Just want to make sure you heard it." Looking over the small wall alongside their booth, he glanced toward where the kitchen was. "Our food should be out soon. You want to speed this up?"

"It's easier if we practice while dining," she said.

"Listen, you're here to give lessons, not make sure I take them. So you eat proper-like. I'll eat like I eat and watch you do it your way. I'd watch you do anything with your sexy mouth."

"You're going to make everything difficult, aren't you?" she asked, somehow feeling up to the challenge.

Giving her the most audacious look, he shook his head. "Mmm, not all things."

His meaning was clear and Natasha did her best not to blush. She couldn't remember any man pursuing her so hard, which was a feat considering she was come on to a lot. The waitress saved her from answering by bringing their food. True to his word, Roark ate like a man, which was to say he ate with relish, taking huge bites and over-salting everything. His glass seemed to travel around his plate, landing wherever he felt like placing it.

If he wasn't willing to listen to her lessons, she decided that she'd merely show by example, taking little, delicate bites. He made small talk, refusing to mention the proposal for sex that hung between them. But it was there, nearly palpable and as heady as the feelings inside her body. Natasha hated to admit it, but there was something animalistic and sensual about the way he attacked his meal with gusto. Would he attack everything in such a manner?

Halfway through the meal she knew she'd most

likely take him up on his offer. By the end of the meal she was sure of it. Roark was smart, sexy, witty and, most importantly, eager to fulfill every desire she had.

Vibrator or Roark? It wasn't a hard call.

Wait, could she choose both?

She shivered. Desire boiled just below her surface. After the meal, Roark threw money down on the table to pay for it.

"My company can pay for my lunch," she assured him. "It's the perk of having an expense account."

Roark stood, reaching to help her up. As his hand slid into hers, he grinned. "But if your company paid for your meal, you wouldn't let me count this as a first date. And if this isn't a date, then how will I justify asking for a kiss at the end of it? Or inviting you in for wine and a massage?"

"Bye, Roark, you sweetie pie you!" the hostess yelled from behind the counter. He smiled angelically at the woman, waving back at her.

"You are impossible, Mr. O'Connell," Natasha said, eyeing the busty hostess.

"Mmm, you have no idea, *a thaisce*."

## 3

Natasha stared at Roark's ass pressed against the leather seat of his bike as she followed him back to his house for more etiquette lessons. It seemed ridiculous at this point, as it was clear he didn't want to learn and had no pressing reason to listen to anything she had to teach him. Oddly, she found his lack of perfect manners refreshing. After working with hoity-toity celebrities and their model-perfect wives, Roark's laid-back approach to life was appealing.

*Speaking of appealing...*

His jacket and T-shirt flapped in the wind, giving peeks of his naked back. She wondered how she should start her next lesson. And what exactly should that lesson be? Roark would undoubtedly go for a "hey, come over here and fuck me wild" line, but Natasha couldn't force herself to say it.

*Dancing? Perhaps. That will get us close enough together to let nature take its course.*

*Interviewing? Ugh, no, not interviewing. Though if I asked the right questions... Wait, no. Too obvious.*

*Clothing? No, that would require shopping and I want to "stay in" to see if he'll continue his bold seduction.*

"Just play it cool, Natasha," she said, looking in the rearview mirror. Grabbing for her purse, she dug inside to find some blush and started putting it on while driving, along with some fresh lipstick. Then, taking her perfume, she sprayed herself, making sure to get between her thighs.

It was too bad she couldn't take her hair down into a much more seductive style without being obvious. As much as she wanted him sexually, she wanted him to continue to ask her for it. She knew she was going to give in to him. But he didn't need to know that. Not yet. "That's right. Just play it cool."

## 4

"DAMN IT, Roark, quit pressuring her. Be cool, man, be cool. Let her come to you." Roark sighed as his house finally came into view. Maybe he should have suggested they go somewhere public. Why did he ask her back to his place? "Because you want her."

He stopped his bike in front of his house, taking a deep breath in an effort to keep his desire at bay.

"Great, talking to myself can't be a good sign. The woman is driving me crazy with lust."

*Shut up, man, or she'll think you've lost it and run.*

Swinging his leg over the back of his bike, he climbed off the motorcycle. Natasha stepped out of her car. Instantly, he detected perfume on the breeze and smiled. She'd put on more makeup too. That had to mean something, right? The beast in him tried to surface.

*Be cool, man, be cool.*

*Shit, she's fucking sexy.*

His cock had never really gone down, even as they made small talk over lunch. As if it had a will of its own, it kept sending thoughts into his head.

*Ask her to suck me dry*, it would say. *Let me fuck that mouth of hers. Come on, take her, you know her pussy's going to feel so good and tight. Can't you smell how wet she is for us? Ah, come on, big fella, you know you want to.*

*Great, not only am I talking to myself, my cock is joining in the conversation as well.*

*She's looking at you. Be cool, man, be cool.*

The sweet, fresh scent of her perfume wrapped around his senses as he neared her, mingling with the already familiar smell of her body's cream. He tried to make his lips move into an easy smile, but it was hard to be easygoing when he fought desire and his inner beast at the same time.

Joining her on the sidewalk leading up to his house, he flipped through his keys to find the one to his front door. Once he had it open, he stepped aside, letting her go in first. He leaned over, looking at the sway of her hips as she went past him. Roark bit his lip to suppress a moan.

*Fuck! I am going to be the first man killed by propriety.*

"How long have you lived here?" she asked.

*Good, light conversation. You can do light. Be cool.*

"Ah, honestly, I can't remember. I tend to move around a lot."

"Restless spirit?"

"Something like that."

"I don't think you ever told me what you do for a living." Natasha finally turned, looking at him. Damn, her eyes were the bluest he'd ever seen. He wished she'd take down her hair for him, so he could see the full richness of the red silky texture.

"It depends on where I'm at," he said.

"What was your last job?"

Roark tensed, not wanting to lie to her, but unable to tell her the truth. Somehow he figured "tracking down and killing rogue werewolves for his father, king of the O'Connell clan" would sound a little crazy to her, if not downright terrifying.

"Let's see, I did some modeling a while back for an erotic novel cover. The book was featured in a magazine."

"Really?"

Was he mistaken or did she look intrigued by that? "Do you read erotic novels?"

The woman actually blushed.

"Interesting," he murmured, his voice low. "So there is a wild side in you waiting to get out."

"And what else have you done?" she asked quickly, refusing to answer.

*Viciously killed a lycan who was hunting children. We regulate our own.*

"Um..." He stepped closer to her. She didn't back away. "I had a stint as a male dancer."

"At the diner?" she laughed.

"No, before that," he said.

"Ballroom?" she asked, her eyes darting down over his body.

"No. Stripper."

"Ah." The sound was a mere squeak. The intense outpouring of her desire filled his nostrils. "That's an, ah, interesting, ah, job."

"Mmm, I'd be more than happy to show you sometime."

"You would?" Again, her voice was weak. Her breathing deepened and her cheeks became flushed as she looked at his chest, only to let her gaze roam lower to where his arousal proudly pressed against his tight leather pants. How he wished she would reach forward and free his hard erection!

"Sit down," he ordered softly, nodding toward the couch. She hesitated, but did as he commanded. Going to a remote, he dimmed the lights and shut the curtains. Then, hitting another button, he slowly walked into the now dark living room as the opening beats of a techno song played. He kept his gaze on her, letting the liquid heat shine in their depths. It didn't matter if it was the middle of the afternoon. Inside the house, the mood was perfect.

Natasha's rounded eyes looked up at him, as if shocked and surprised that he was actually going to dance for her. Slowly, he thrust his hips to the rhythm of the club music. Roark had never been one for a routine but instead he went with the flow of things. The beat picked up and he began moving in time to it, thrusting his hips hard as he artfully worked off his leather jacket. Knowing just how to seduce her by the subtle reactions of her body, he lifted his T-shirt, giving teasing peeks of flesh as he danced closer to her.

He kept the teasing up for a while, kicking off his boots and socks. Then, rolling his stomach and flexing his chest, he ripped the T-shirt back. Natasha gasped, her hands digging into the arm of his couch as she stared at him. The tattered shirt fell to the floor and he kicked it at her. It slid onto her lap, but she didn't take it.

Roark ran his finger along his low waistline, rocking his hips in hard thrusts to keep time with the music. He unbuttoned the pants, working closer to her. Anticipation curled in his gut. This would be a day Natasha never forgot.

❧

NATASHA COULDN'T BREATHE. Roark's sexy dance was doing things to her she never thought could happen and her body was elevated to a mindless state of pure arousal. Squirming in her seat, she was sure her body was so wet that it was soaking his couch. She clenched her thighs together, but the throbbing in her clit didn't stop. The desire she felt from that first moment, the pounding heat that coursed through her blood, made her behave as she might not normally. What was it about this man? The pure animal magnetism she couldn't resist, didn't really want to.

Muscles rippled erotically under his flesh as he moved—and *oh*! did he know how to move. Roark danced closer, until his toned stomach was in her face. Her hands itched to touch him, but she was too afraid to move. There was something all too primal about this man. He was like a caged animal on the brink of escaping.

He slowly pulled down his zipper. The thick tip of his cock peeked out at her, straining to be free of its leather confines. When he looked down at her, his lashes fell low over his dark, penetrating gaze. He was breathing hard, though she doubted a man in his fine shape would be worn out from the seductive moves.

Natasha couldn't stop her hands from reaching forward. His body still rocked in time to the music, though not as aggressively as before. She touched his hips, letting her fingers slide on the warm leather. Roark drew closer, swaying his cock back and forth, moving it toward her lips in silent meaning.

She slid her hands around to cup his ass. It was firm and tight beneath her fingers. Dipping along the back of his thighs, she scooted to the edge of the couch. His scent engulfed her and his heat seemed to jump off his skin onto hers. The leather pants clung to him. She pulled at the material, slowly working it off his hips. His cock seemed to lengthen more as it was freed.

Natasha looked up at him. The dim lights

revealed the contrast between the rise and fall of muscles on his body. Roark reached for her face, stroking her cheek. His eyes pleaded with her to suck him off, but he didn't make a move to force her.

It was more than she could resist. With a moan, she leaned forward, opening her mouth to pull the thick tip of his erection between her lips. She kissed him gently, twirling her tongue around the ridge. He groaned in approval. She pulled back, teasing him as she nibbled her teeth up and down the sides before latching on to him once more. Her hands glided over the leather, caressing his perfect thighs.

Damn, he tasted good!

Natasha sucked him a little deeper. The techno music continued, the beat changing slightly. She kept rhythm, rolling her tongue along his shaft, rimming the firm ridge in circles.

"Ah, *a thaisce*, you look so sexy like that," he said. She saw his stomach tighten as his breath caught. "So prim and proper in your suit and bun, and yet your gorgeous lips just beg to be fucked. It's a huge turn-on."

Natasha moaned, her mouth full of his cock. Her lips moved faster, sucking harder. Roark continued to talk, seemingly unashamed as he vocalized how sexy she was, how hot she made him, how he wanted to come down in her lovely throat and watch her drink him up.

He pumped his hips forward, slipping deeper until he hit the back of her mouth. She kept her hands on his hips, trying to set the pace while enjoying the feel of his trim body. Roark grabbed his extra length, running his fist over what she couldn't fit. Her lips hit his fist and she couldn't help but stare at the exotic sight of watching him jack off as she sucked him.

"Ah, shit!" Roark growled. "Oh, yeah, baby, just like that. Take me in deep. Get me nice and wet with that sweet mouth of yours. *Mmm!*"

Roark stiffened, grunting as he came hard. She drank down his seed, loving the salty-sweet taste of him. Natasha pulled back, looking up.

Grabbing her by the arms, Roark pulled her to her feet in front of him. "I can't believe I haven't kissed you yet."

Before she could respond, his mouth captured hers. He moaned, exploring the depths of her mouth with his tongue—probing, tasting, conquering. Roark pressed his body to hers and she felt his thick arousal against her. He was still hard and ready.

How in the world...?

Lightheaded, she pulled her mouth from his. "Roark..."

"Shh, *a thaisce*," he murmured along her throat as he nipped at her fervent pulse. "Just go with it."

In the back of her mind, she wondered how he retained his size after such a hard orgasm. His kisses felt so good, she couldn't form a coherent thought. The man was more than well-endowed and her jaw ached from the thickness of him.

"There is just something about you," he admitted. "Since I first saw you standing on my porch, I can't seem to think of anything but you."

"It's only been a few hours," she reminded him.

"Doesn't matter. You're amazing."

Roark jerked her suit jacket off her shoulders. The cooler air hit her through the silk, instantly bringing relief to her overheated body. Suddenly, he grabbed her around the waist and hoisted her up on his shoulder. Natasha squealed as he carted her off in caveman fashion down the hall. He maneuvered easily around the boxes.

His hands roamed over the back of her legs as he walked and his breathing was harsh. Turning a corner, he brought her to a darkened room. She shivered, unable to see. Just as she was about to ask where they were, she was tossed into the air. Yelping in surprise, she landed on her back on a soft feather-top mattress. A cotton comforter molded to her body. The bed shifted with Roark's weight and she reached for him, instantly hitting a naked thigh in the dark. She ran her hand along the curve of his ass. He'd taken off the pants.

"Your stockings have to go," he said, his voice thick. It would seem whenever he was highly aroused, his voice would develop a softened burr to his words, reminiscent of a light Irish accent.

Natasha lay on her back. Suddenly, his hand dove up her skirt, only to hold on to her inner thigh. She wasn't sure how he managed so smoothly, but he ran his finger down her leg, ripping the material with his nail. Her heels were still on her feet and he left them as he reached her ankles. Delving up her skirt again, he ripped her hose on the other side.

"Mmm, much better." Sitting between her legs, he lifted a foot and slid off her shoe. He kissed her toes, working his way up her foot to her leg, removing the tattered stocking from her leg as he went—nibbling, biting, soothing. An animalistic growl sounded in the back of his throat, primitive and raw. When he reached her inner thigh, he began the process over with her other foot, kissing up her leg, flicking his tongue over her heated flesh.

She wished she could see his face, but the darkness hid him from view. He slid his hands along flesh, ridding her of the tattered stockings completely. Roark breathed lightly on her flesh, settling between her thighs. She tried to close her knees, but he growled, shoving them back open.

Her skirt was around her waist, leaving her vulnerable to his whims. Roark moaned, kissing the crease where her inner thigh met her hip. Natasha was suddenly very glad she'd decided to wear lace panties that morning.

"So wet," he whispered, rubbing his face along her panties. Nails scraped along her panty line, coming to her crotch. Pulling, he cut through the material. "So hot."

"How...?" she asked, only to gasp as his warm lips covered her aching bud.

Very few men had ventured down on her and none had enjoyed doing it as much as Roark obviously did. He groaned in pleasure, tasting her and showing no shame in enjoying it. Her body shook with pleasure, as it flowed from her pussy over her limbs, encircling her hard nipples. She grabbed her breasts, arching her hips for more. The silk of her shirt slid over her lace bra. He nicked her with his teeth, only to suck and lick the playful wound.

As his tongue slipped down over her folds, holding them open, she felt it reach inside her. She gasped, feeling him lick her intimately. The man knew how to wiggle his tongue, fast and hard and deep, as he found the sweet spot hidden in her depths.

Natasha rode his mouth, as he tongue-fucked her. His groans turned to primal growls, like a beast dining on flesh. He became more aggressive, nicking her with his teeth, reaching higher into her depths. Fingernails gripped into her thighs, holding her open as wide as her legs could spread. Desperate, she reached above her head, gripping the soft comforter.

His mouth moved back up her slit to find the hard bundle of nerves hidden along her top arch. As he thrust a thick finger into her pussy to replace his hot tongue, he worked it back and forth, only to pull it back out when it was wet with her cream. Boldly, and without any hesitation, he drew his finger down to the tight rosette between her cheeks, pressing against her virgin ass. Natasha cried out in surprise, gasping as he rimmed her anus.

"Ah, shit." His voice was raspy and urgent. "You've never been taken here, have you?"

She shook her head.

"How is it possible with an ass as nice as yours?

Don't worry, love, you're with a real man now. I'll show you what you've been missing. I'm going to fuck this ass of yours real good."

The revelation only seemed to arouse him more. He pushed his finger deeper, sending intense shock waves through her at the forbidden touch. Growling, he renewed his attention on her pussy, fucking her with his tongue and finger in both openings. Soon another finger joined the first, and then a third, working her, stretching her, preparing her ass for his cock.

Natasha moaned weakly, helpless, as he had his way with her. Nothing in her life had felt like this. Old sensations, ones she needed to suppress, tried to surge forth. She denied them, only accepting the pleasure he gave and not making anything more out of what was happening. Her stomach tightened and she cried out in surprise as her orgasm hit her like a sudden burst of flames, making her hot and cold at once. Her only answer was his growl. He continued to move, stroking her, until he'd milked every tremor from her body. When her legs fell weakly onto the bed, he finally pulled back.

## 5

Roark sat back on the bed. He saw Natasha easily in the darkness, as he pierced it with his inborn lycan vision. It was clear by the look on her face that she couldn't see him. He was glad. It was why he brought her to the dark bedroom. The beast within him wanted to play, and play it had, coming to the surface as she rode his hand and mouth.

Damn, but her ass was so tight, squeezing down on him as he thrust into it.

His cock was full, straining for attention. The problem was, in his state of desire it had grown larger than before. Humans were fragile, not meant to take the beast. Sure, there were a few who could, mostly of the porn star persuasion, but Natasha was no porn star.

What would she do if she saw him half shifted? Would she be into it? Would she scream and run away from him? No, it was better to leave her in the dark for now. Let her trust him first, and then he'd show her.

"Roark?" she whispered. "Is everything all right?"

He realized he'd been dead quiet, not moving and not touching her in an effort to regain control. "Yeah, *a thaisce*."

"I like it when you call me that," she admitted. The shyness in her tone would be his undoing. He reached for her, rubbing his hand up her leg. "What does it mean?"

"My treasure," he said absently. His hand had a single-minded purpose as he reached up to her breast. She still wore her shirt. Without thinking, he grabbed it and ripped it open. Buttons flew and he heard the faintest pings as they landed on the floor. Then, easily shifting a tiny bit to grow a claw at the end of his fingertip, he sliced her bra down the middle, freeing her surprisingly large breasts. The bra had hidden their true size from him. He didn't care about the clothing. He could well afford to replace anything he destroyed. As fast as it came, the claw disappeared.

Roark licked his lips, narrowing in on her body's response as he touched a naked breast. A shiver worked over her, sprinkling her flesh with goose bumps. Mesmerized, he leaned forward and gently brushed his mouth across her erect nipple.

Natasha arched on the bed, thrusting her breast at his mouth. He flicked his tongue over her nipples, alternating passionately between the two, hardening them. Roark moaned, as if feeling the life-force in her as he touched her. A light energy seemed to hum between them, but he knew it was only his imagination, his strong need to mark her with his scent.

Crawling above her, he captured her lips, careful to keep his fangs from poking her. His heart skipped around in his chest and he probed her mouth as he had her pussy, sipping her taste and testing her response. He sucked her tongue into his mouth and urged her to explore inside him as he did her.

Sitting back on his heels, he heard her gasp at the sudden departure. He breathed deeply, trying to go slow, trying to regain the control that threatened to slip from him. Everything about her hit him like a drug. "Your scent has been driving me crazy."

"My...ah, scent?"

Roark bit back a laugh, and lied to put her at ease. "The perfume you're wearing."

"Oh."

He grabbed her parted thighs and pulled her toward him so her legs straddled the sides of his. Letting his hand roam across her full lips, he drew his fingers over her neck, across the rapid pulse he found there, to her chest. He tweaked her nipples, rolling each of them between his thumb and forefinger. Continuing across her flat stomach, he moved his hand between her thighs to stroke along her slick folds. When his finger was wet with her cream, he brought it to his lips and licked it. His other hand tightened on her thigh as he savored her taste.

Natasha pushed up from the bed and reached for him, running her hands over his chest. He let her explore him as she blindly felt her way down to his erection. Watching her closely as she wrapped her fingers around his now incredibly thick length, he saw her eyes round in surprise. Taking him in both hands, she touched his erection, feeling the veins along the shaft, seeming to measure the thickness with her palm even as she felt the long length.

"Roark?" she asked, weakly. "Did you... Have you gotten... Did you take a pill or something to make your...make it bigger?"

A pill? He did his best not to laugh.

"I told you, love, you do something to me." He

cupped his balls, rolling them in his palm as she continued searching his length in awe. Her hands looked so small compared to his. He bit his lip, drawing blood with a fang. Lightly, she fingered the mushroomed tip, even stopping to push at the small hole on the end filled with pre-cum. Roark tried to hold back, but he couldn't. His penis surged, growing slightly bigger. Natasha gasped, pulling her hands away, and he could just imagine her telling herself that she would never fit him inside her.

"I want you to fuck me," she said, her voice throaty and low.

Roark was too stunned to speak.

Natasha pulled the tattered remains of her shirt off her arms and tossed it aside. Then, getting on her hands and knees, she presented her lush ass to him. "Come on, wild man. Do it. Give me your big cock. Make me take it all."

With a growl, he surged forward. She didn't know what she was asking for. He stroked her back, coming between her parted legs. Cream glistened over her mound, a testament to how ready she was for him. He touched her wet folds and she jolted with liquid excitement. He thrust into her tight passage with his finger, loosening the silken muscles of her pussy.

"I want you to break me open," she told him, pushing back on his hand. "Give me all of it. Make me scream. Please, Roark, fuck me like you promised to do. It's been so long since I've been taken."

When his fingers were moist with her cream, he ran them down between the cheeks of her ass, teasing the rosette he found there. He probed the tight muscles with a finger, rimming her gently.

"Yes, there. Fuck me there as well." Natasha pulled at her hair. Silken red waves fell over her shoulders. "Come on, biker boy. Take me for a ride."

If it had been anyone else, he would have laughed, but coming from Natasha it was just too damned hot. He groaned, pulling his finger away, unable to take the torture.

Grabbing his cock, he rubbed the tip along her slit. Natasha panted her approval, spreading her legs wider for him, inviting him in. She leaned to the side, grabbing and pinching a nipple. A hot gush of liquid flowed from her, easing his way.

"So sweet," he managed, though it didn't do justice to the thoughts running through his head. Then, he could think of nothing as he thrust into her slick folds, prying her pussy open with his stiff mass. She gasped, her tight body gripping him hard. He had to pull back, stretching her by small degrees. The beast fought for mindless control, but he forced it down. Sliding in her natural juices, he moved back and forth in shallow thrusts, pushing deeper into her, stretching her tight pussy to fit him.

"I said, fuck me!" Natasha demanded. She thrust herself back, impaling herself on his full length. Her body clamped him so tight it was almost painful. She screamed. Roark tensed in concern. Before he could speak, she yelled, "Yes. That's it. Give it to me."

Roark let loose a primal cry of pleasure. Instantly, he began thrusting, pounding his thick cock into her hot channel. Natasha yelled for more, demanding he give it all to her. He did give it all, and then some. Grabbing her hips, he pulled open the cleft of her ass, parting her even more. The more the beast came to play, the more she screamed in approval.

"Roark! Roark!" she cried, saying his name over and over. "Yes, Roark!"

He leaned back for leverage. The act of straightening his upper body drove his hips forward so he was deeper still. His muscles strained as he pumped faster. Glorious pressure built in him. With a growl, his body began to tighten. He reached for her clit, stroking the bud as he continued to control her movements by her hip.

Natasha gasped, her body stiffening. Roark

thrust deep, stopping inside her. Her muscles tightened around him, convulsing along his embedded shaft. Screaming, she arched her body before him. He tried to hold back, tried to keep from ejaculating, but it was no use. His seed shot into her, marking her with his scent and draining him. He wasn't worried about diseases. As a lycan, he couldn't get them and thus couldn't give them. And, unless she was his mate, she wouldn't get pregnant. Still embedded, he leaned his head against her back.

Natasha collapsed onto the bed. Roark fell to her side. His eyes closed and he knew he'd soon be asleep.

"Rest up, sweetheart," Natasha whispered. "I'm not done with you yet."

## 6

"Roark!"

Natasha blinked, opening her eyes. Her whole body was numb with pleasure and she must have fallen asleep. Looking next to her on the bed, she noticed that Roark was gone. A thin strip of light caught her attention, giving just the tiniest bit of light to see by. It came from beneath a door. She was on a king-size bed with four dark posters in each corner and a wooden canopy up top. The shadowed impression of an oversized wardrobe was along the wall.

"Roark?" The sound was closer. Suddenly, the door to the bedroom was thrown open. "Damn it, Roark, get your lazy ass out of bed. I won the bet. You slept in..."

As soon as the light was turned on, the man

stopped talking. Natasha screeched in embarrassment, grabbing at the covers to hide her nudity. The man at the door looked like Roark, though he was taller. His hair was the same dark shade, instead of the long locks that had tickled her during sex, his were short, falling just to his chin. He wore a faded pair of blue jeans and a white T-shirt with bright orange writing advertising an old-fashioned type of soda on it.

"Damn it, James!" Roark yelled. He stood in the doorway leading to a master bathroom, looking as if he'd just gotten out of the shower with a towel wrapped around his waist. It was the same door that gave her the little bit of light to see by when she first woke up. "Get out of here! She doesn't want you ogling her."

Roark launched a brush at James' head. His brother ducked out of the room and the brush hit the wall with a loud bang.

"Sorry 'bout him," Roark said, striding to the bed. He looked at her, the kind of intimate look men got after sex. She blushed and started to hide her face. "He's the one in need of manners training, obviously. Though I'll be damned if I let him use you for it. You're all mine, love."

Natasha laughed. Roark hopped up on the bed and kissed her, moaning into her mouth.

"Rummage though the drawers, boxes, wherever and find something to wear. I'm going to make us something to eat."

Natasha nodded. Whistling, Roark walked to a box, grabbed a pair of blue jeans and dropped the towel. Without breaking stride, he walked naked out of the bedroom. She stared at his ass as he closed the door.

Moaning, she fell over on the bed and buried her face in a pillow.

## 7

"I can't believe it," James drawled as Roark sauntered into his kitchen to find something to eat. He was leaning against the countertop. "You got Ms. Manners into bed within hours. It makes me want to hire an etiquette coach."

Roark knew his brother was only teasing him, but he still didn't like him being so cavalier about what had happened between Natasha and him. There was no way James could know how deeply he felt for the woman.

Forcing a chuckle, he tossed his jeans over a chair and didn't bother to get dressed. It was his house and he would walk around naked if he felt like it. After centuries, James would hardly be fazed by his brother's nudity. During full shifts, they all lost their clothes. Pointing at his brother, he warned, "She's all mine, so back off."

James laughed, holding his hands out to his sides. "Ah, so the connection I sensed between you two is real. By all means, Roark, keep her. I don't share with my brothers."

"What? No lecture like you gave Ian about Meghan?" Roark rummaged through his fridge, pulling out a carton of eggs and some cheese.

"I was right about Meghan," James said. Meghan had been Ian's lover for years. Though Ian wanted nothing more than sex, the woman had her sights on being queen. She wasn't happy when Ian chose Ceana. She even went so far as striking a deal with a sea witch to get Ceana out of the way. Her plan failed and she was now on the run.

"Any luck tracking her down?" Roark asked.

"No, but I have word she's in Las Vegas." James shrugged. "I wanted to talk to you and Ian about the best way to handle her before I left, but Ian called to say they found a place in Virginia that Ceana wants to look at first before they come here."

"Meghan betrayed our brother," Roark reminded him. "What is there to discuss? You track her and punish her for her crimes."

"And she failed in her plotting," James answered.

"Without power, she's harmless. The whole clan is ready to turn her in for what she did. Besides, Father already ordered me to hold back a week before going after her. He wants her to get comfortable and settled in to her new home."

"A week?"

"That's what he said." James shot him a mischievous look. "So I guess I'll be staying with you, brother. No reason to waste away at the hotel."

"Oh, no," Roark said glancing in the direction of his bedroom. He could hear the shower in the master bath running and wished he could make an excuse to jump in with her. "Not this time, buddy. I've got plans and they don't include escorting you to the emergency room like last time."

"You're going to kick your brother out on his ass for a woman?" James gasped, pretending to be stunned. "You're going to make me spend a whole week in a hotel by my lonesome?"

"For that woman? Hell, yes! In fact, you're already overstaying your welcome. Get out of here." Roark knew James was only giving him a hard time. They stayed much longer in hotels when out on a job. "Quit whining. You don't even own a house, do you?"

"Can't remember. I think I own a couple." James

pushed away from the counter and grabbed the carton of eggs from Roark's hand. "One thing though, if I leave right now, who's going to do the cooking? You?"

"I can..." It wasn't even worth finishing the lie. "Fine, you can stay. But just for breakfast."

"Gee, thanks."

"Then it's back to the hotel. I want some time alone with Natasha and she's only guaranteed me a week." Roark grinned, turning toward his bedroom, still naked. Unashamed, he planned on leaving James alone in the kitchen to attend some unfinished business he had with Natasha.

"Hey," James yelled. "You're not going to leave me to do the cooking all alone, are you?"

"Sorry, old chap, but yeah I am!" Roark hurried to the bedroom, shutting the door quietly behind him.

## 8

ROARK STRODE toward the master bathroom, smiling as he heard Natasha humming softly in the shower. It felt right having her in his home, as if she'd been there forever. He pushed his hair over his shoulder, not caring that he'd just taken a shower and the locks were still damp.

Suddenly, he was feeling very, very dirty. Grabbing his semi-erect shaft, Roark pumped his fist over the length until it became hard.

He stopped in the doorway, watching the blurred image of Natasha's beautiful body through the thick glass door. There was more than enough room for both of them in the shower and he eagerly went toward her. Letting his cock slide along the cool glass, he said, "Want some company?"

He lifted upon his toes to see over the shower door. Natasha gasped, spinning around. Wet hair clung to her lightly tanned skin. Her round blue eyes fluttered in the overspray of water as she blinked rapidly, staring at where his penis pressed to the glass. Roark's gaze narrowed in on her wet breasts. Rivulets trailed down her supple flesh, coming from the two showerheads on either side of her body.

"Isn't your brother here?" she asked, her eyes darting up to meet his.

"So what if he is. He'll stay away."

"I should say no."

Roark rocked his hips against the hard glass. Letting his expression fill with his desire for her, he murmured, "But you want to say yes."

"Yes."

Grinning, he pulled open the door and joined her. Hot water hit his body and steam curled around them. She fell forward onto his chest, moaning in pleasure. Instantly, he pulled her into his arms, kissing her thoroughly as their flesh rubbed together with the aid of the shower. Her hands slipped over his chest and arms, as if trying to feel all of him at once. Not to be outdone, Roark explored her as well, teasing and probing, reading her body's reaction to continue doing what she liked the best.

Her mouth slid off his, licking water from his flesh. Her hot tongue flicked over his pulse before she worked her mouth down to his chest. Roark groaned when she sucked one of his nipples into her mouth. She pulled back.

"Roark, *shhh*. Your brother will hear." Her expectant face looked up at him in concern.

"Mmm, is this a lesson in shower sex etiquette?" He grinned, unable to resist teasing her.

"Well, Mr. O'Connell, you know, there are certain rules that one must abide by."

"Really?" He reached to lightly brush the back of his hand along her soft curls. She shivered as he skimmed her clit. "What are those?"

"Uh," she giggled, "ladies first."

"I think I can manage that," he assured her, gracefully going to his knees before her. Sticking out his tongue, he rubbed it along her slit, parting her folds with the tip.

❧

NATASHA WASN'T sure how he did it, but Roark was absolutely, hands-down the best lover she'd ever had. It was in the confidence of his movements, the graceful flex of his body. It was in the way he tasted, the way he conquered her lips with his when he kissed her. One look could leave her knees weak and one touch could melt her with desire.

She moaned lightly, looking down at his dark head between her thighs. Rich, silky waves of hair adhered to his strong flesh. Water beat against her, caressing like a million fingers at once. Her nipples were hard peaks beneath the hard stream of water. Jerking waves of pleasure flowed over her skin. His mouth sawed passionately against her, instantly weakening her knees.

Roark looked up, his dark eyes piercing, watching her, wanting her. She grabbed his head, leaning back as she arched toward his mouth. An orgasm hit her hard, causing her to convulse wildly.

Roark shot to his feet and Natasha felt the hard pressure of his tight body all along hers. The water slid between them, making his hard muscles glide erotically along her softer form. His thick arousal settled against her stomach, hotter than the water. Then, his eyes met hers. They were no longer dark brown flecked with hints of gold. The amber color had taken over completely.

Gasping, she pushed back in the shower. "Roark?"

He closed his eyes. His hands were on her hips,

gripping her. His tone hoarse, he said, "It will pass. Please, don't be frightened. I won't hurt you. I'm the same man I was before. Please, just—"

Natasha wasn't frightened. She surged forward, pressing her lips to his. It was his turn to gasp in surprise. Moaning, she forced her tongue into his mouth. Sharpened teeth nicked her and Roark instantly started sucking on her like a man starved.

Fangs? His eyes? What was this man?

Natasha knew well that the supernatural truly existed. She herself had been part of that world before she was doomed to become human. Strange, she'd lost all her other powers, but she'd just assumed she'd know another supernatural if she saw one. She had Roark pegged as a human male—a deliciously sculpted one, but human nonetheless.

"What kind are you?" she asked, breathing heavily. "You're too dark to be vampire. Shifter? Warlock?"

He pulled back, clearly surprised by her acceptance and curiosity. "You know of my kind?"

"Then you are a warlock?" she asked, astonished. She wouldn't have taken him for the old magical kind.

"No. Lycan."

"Now that makes more sense." He had the brute

strength and the vitality of the werewolf and the passionate intensity of a shifter. It also explained the size of his anatomy and how it seemed to grow.

"You are familiar with lycans?" he asked, still eyeing her in disbelief. "And you're not scared?"

"I've met a few over my lifetime," she assured him. Natasha moaned, turned on even more now that she knew his secret. The fierce, animal look of him, the knowledge of what he kept buried inside him. It was all a turn-on. No wonder she couldn't resist his sexual charms. He wasn't a mere human, he was base animalistic desire and passion wrapped up into a perfect male package. The urge to tell him the truth welled within her, but she couldn't think beyond passion to say the words.

"Turn around," he ordered, the sound of the beast in his low voice. Grabbing her ass, he squeezed it hard. "I'm going to finish what I started. I'm going to conquer all of you."

Natasha shivered, but how could she refuse such a passionate request? Turning, she braced her hands against the wall, spreading her legs. Roark came from behind, running his hands up over her thighs, caressing her. His harsh breathing sounded over her. "I love that you know what I am," he said. "I hate deception."

Natasha wanted to speak, wanted to tell him all about herself, but now wasn't the time. He pressed his body along hers, rubbing it up and down. His thick arousal settled between the cheeks of her ass, as he pressed her tight against the wall. The hard shower wall kept her trapped, but Roark managed to slip his hands between it and her breasts. He massaged them, taking the full globes in his hands, letting the rougher texture of his wet palms move over her nipples. His hands explored her, commanding her flesh as he boldly touched wherever he desired. She was surrounded by him—his tight body to her back, his hands on her front. He rocked his hips to her, growling in pleasure as he kissed the back of her neck.

"Mmm," Natasha moaned, shivering in excitement and anticipation.

He bit her shoulder, but not hard enough to break the skin. His dangerous fangs skimmed her flesh as if any moment he'd bear down and drink her blood. Leaning back, she reached behind her head to try and touch him. It was of little use. Roark had complete control of her body and she could only take the pleasure he gave her.

Animalistic sounds of possession came from him,

vibrating against her. "I want to bury myself deep inside you."

Natasha nodded weakly, closing her eyes as his hand slid between her thighs from behind. She trembled in anticipation. He took his cock in hand and wiggled the tip around her folds to find entrance. Grabbing her leg, he pulled her knee up, opening her body wide as he let the tip probe just inside her pussy.

Her body was wet, more than ready. She wanted him. Her hips bucked in offering and he chuckled hotly next to her ear. "Soon, love, soon."

Slowly, he thrust up, filling her pussy as he slid to the hilt inside her. Plunging a few times, he lubed himself before slipping back to the tight rosette entrance of her ass. With so much control that it drove her mad, he pushed into her tight passage, filling her body by small, agonizing degrees. Nerves jumped along her spine, spreading warmth and delight throughout her frame.

Her eyes rolled back in her head and she gasped for air. The shower hit her, caressing like millions of fingers, heightening the pleasure. His thick cock stretched her wide, prying her ass open. She felt so full, her ass burning in pleasure. Seating himself to the hilt, he paused, letting her body adjust to him.

Natasha gasped for breath as gratification radiated over her.

"Ah, *a thaisce*." Roark groaned. Holding her up with ease, he moved inside her ass. He licked and teased her neck as his hips pulled back only to thrust in shallow strokes. His hands grabbed hers, pressing them to the wall as he held her down before him. Her leg slid down, squeezing his cock tight between her ass cheeks.

"Ah, Roark," she moaned. "Roark."

At her words, he thrust harder, faster. She screamed in mindless pleasure, feeling warmth in the pit of her stomach. It was power, an old familiar power she hadn't felt for a long time. Her breasts tingled, so alive, so achy with passion. Her pussy clenched as he worked back and forth in her ass.

Natasha was glad that the wall held her up, as her legs weakened. She started to shake, jerking violently as Roark grunted wildly. His long dark hair stuck to her flesh, mingling with her own. He stroked up, hitting hard into her tight passage.

"*A thaisce, a thaisce*," he groaned in her ear, over and over as if punctuating each thrust with those words. "*A thaisce*."

He rocked himself into her with a violent force, conquering her entire depths. The pleasure built inside her body. She was close, so close. Slipping his hand between her and the wall, he tweaked her clit, rubbing it in tight circles. Natasha's whole body went rigid as she instantly came. Growling, Roark fucked her faster, harder, deeper, seating himself until he had no more to give.

Her body convulsed around his hard shaft as the strong force of her orgasm hit her and tears came to her eyes from the pure intensity of the moment. Roark stiffened, as he jerked his cum into her ass. They stood frozen in time, her body helpless against the wall as he kept his cock buried deep inside her.

Natasha tingled from head to toe, partly because of the intense pleasure of release and partly due to the old feeling of magic in her limbs. The first time they came together, she'd held back. But had knowing his secret, knowing he was supernatural, made her lose her hold on her feelings? As reason dawned on her, she wiggled to be free.

How could the magic be back? How, unless...?

The shower stopped running, the water freezing in mid-air, not like ice, just stopped in time. Silence surrounded them. She felt Roark moving behind her, as if looking around in confusion. Natasha didn't move.

"Bravo, cousin." The deeply amused voice was punctuated by slow clapping.

Natasha gasped. Roark jerked out of her ass and turned toward the shower door, trying to put his body protectively between her and the intruder.

"Roark, don't," she whispered, touching his arm as he threatened to shift. She smoothed down the hair that rose on his skin, evidence of his oncoming change. Roark's eyes glowed as they glanced back at her, their yellow orbs terrifying. "Dem, don't! Get out of here."

"You know him?" Roark demanded, his voice gravelly.

"Natasha, as you wish," her cousin said. "I'll just wait in the other room. But you'd better hurry, the family isn't too far behind me."

Suddenly, the shower started again as if it had never stopped. Roark gave the showerhead a passing glance but turned back to study her.

"Natasha?" Roark asked, a frown marring his brow as he looked her up and down.

Natasha followed his gaze. Her skin glittered, shining as if covered by tiny crystals, and she was pale, almost blue in color. Her magic was back, full force. She felt it surging to be freed from her body, but she reeled it in.

"I can explain," she whispered. The shower was still running, and she lifted her hand to shut it off without touching anything but air.

Roark pushed behind him, opening the door. "What's going on? What are you?"

"I'm a farfadet. I was under a spell, a curse of sorts that made me human." Natasha pushed past him to get out of the shower. Looking frantically over the floor, she said, "I was supposed to marry this man and I didn't want to. Since I was the only female, my defiance to find any husband, to even look for one, angered the elders and they banished me to be and live as a human until I was ready to comply. They said if I was going to fumble my way through such things I very well should be mortal.

"At first I was mad, but after finding the freedom of being human to be quite satisfactory, I avoided all things magic. Please don't be mad that I didn't tell you right after I found out you were a lycan. It's just you were touching me and I couldn't think straight. I was going to let you know afterward, only there wasn't time because—" She caught her reflection in the mirror. Her eyes had widened slightly and her ears pointed. Touching her face, she shook her head. "Oh, no, I'm changing back."

"Back to what?" Roark asked carefully, slower to come out of the shower. "A farfadet?"

"Yes, my magic form," she said absently, grabbing a discarded T-shirt off the floor. Frowning, she shook it and it was instantly clean and pressed. She slipped it on. When she pulled her head through the neck hole, her hands were slightly webbed and her nails had grown longer. "Oh, no. No. I thought I was free from all this."

"Natasha?" Roark hesitated, looking her over. Crouching slightly, she stared at him, her stomach pulling in toward her spine. He came to her and she winced. "*Shhh*. It's all right, *a thaisce*."

"You don't understand. I've done something." She shook her head.

"What? What have you done? Whatever it is, I can help. My father is king of the O'Connell clan. He has influence among the magical creatures. He's well respected and I myself have some weight."

"You don't understand what I've done," she repeated.

"What? What have you done? Murder? What crime did you commit to get cursed?"

"No, not to curse me," she began, wanting to explain.

"What?"

"She's married," came a voice from the doorway.

Natasha looked up at her father. It had been years since she'd seen him and her first impulse was to hug him. Then, remembering the last time they met, she held back. They had not parted on good terms. In fact, it was that fight that had turned her human.

"Button," her father said, a sudden smile broke out over his face.

"Father," she whispered. "But you hate using your powers to come to this dimension. What are you doing here? Now? In this time?"

The man turned to Roark, but her lover was too busy staring at her.

"You're married?" Roark asked.

"My son." Her father beamed, holding his arms wide for Roark.

If she thought seeing her turn into magical form had put a look of shock on his face, having her father call him "son" knocked him senseless.

"Natasha?" Roark asked after a long, awkward silence. He didn't move to touch her father's outstretched hands. "What is he talking about?"

"I'm sorry," she whispered. "I should've known they were coming back the second I saw you, but it's been so long since I've used them. I thought it was merely attraction. I held them at bay the first time, but just now when I discovered what you were I let loose of my control and my powers came back when we were... When we were in the middle of... When we were having..."

"Sex," her father supplied nonchalantly.

Natasha made a weak noise. She'd been human for a long time and that included developing some human insecurities her kind normally didn't have—including talking openly about sex in front of her father.

"Father, please," Natasha begged. "You're not helping."

"Sorry, Button." He smiled wider. He turned, holding his arms opened to the side.

"Father, this..." She motioned around. "This is awkward. Please, could we have a moment? I need to explain."

Her father dropped his arms, frowning at Roark. "You reject her?"

"What?" Roark asked.

"It's quite simple," the farfadet elder said. "Did you bind yourself to my daughter?"

"What? No, sir, no. I didn't touch her like that," he swore.

Natasha gasped, her mouth falling open. How

could he so readily deny what was between them? When she felt it more surely than anything else in her life?

"Natasha?" her father asked, no longer happy.

"He didn't do it," she said. "His kind bites." She turned to Roark. "Is that right?"

Roark nodded. "Yes, and we also require an elder's blessing."

"He didn't bite me, Father." Natasha slowly walked to her father. "It was all me."

"I see," her father said. He lifted his hand and cupped her cheek, tears filling his eyes. "I've only just now found you only to lose you again. Come. We must prepare."

"Nat—"

Natasha glanced over her shoulder as Roark's voice was cut off. His image blurred as her father carried her body away from the lycan's home. She saw him charge forward to grab for her. It was too late. The last image she saw of him was his body transforming into lycan as he dove through air.

## 9

ROARK BREATHED HEAVILY, looking at his brother in disbelief as he crashed through the now empty bedroom ready to fight. Desperate, he'd called to him using his mind as the man had taken Natasha from him.

"Shit, what was that?" James demanded. "These little blue and green creatures started buzzing all over the living room like hell-spawned demons—jumping on my head, breaking everything they touched. And then, *bam*! They were gone and everything was exactly as it was before they came."

"Farfadets," Roark said quietly.

"Farfadets? What are they doing in the mortal world? They usually stay with their own kind. It's said they hide in history's pages and can't be found unless one can travel through time to find them."

"James, they took her," Roark said quietly. Just saying the words out loud made a terrible pain rip through his guts.

They took her.

They took Natasha.

They took the woman he loved.

"You love her," James said softly, as if reading his heart.

"Yes, I love her." With the acknowledgement came the bittersweet feeling of hopelessness. Why had he hesitated? When Natasha's father asked him if he was married to her, he didn't lie, did he? He felt connected to her, more than he'd ever been connected to anyone. Did she claim him? Is that what she'd been trying to tell him?

"Who came then?"

"Her father?"

"Whose? The etiquette lady's?"

"Yeah, Natasha's father, the farfadet." Roark knew his answers were mindless, stunned whispers, but he couldn't concentrate. He stared around his room, as if by sheer will he could get her back. His body was tense, half-shifted and naked, but he didn't care. Blood pumped in his veins, filling him with desperation and anger.

"She didn't smell like a farfadet," James said thoughtfully.

"I didn't get the whole story, but apparently, she refused to marry and was turned human as punishment. Somehow, being with me broke the spell, or the curse, or whatever it is that was done to her."

"And I thought the lycan laws were tough." James shook his head, swearing lightly. "You know, it's odd, but first Ian and his cursed mermaid and now you and your cursed farfadet."

Roark frowned. "This is completely different."

"How? Ceana loves Ian and she was a cursed mermaid."

"Exactly, Ceana loves Ian and Ian loves Ceana."

"Oh, so you don't think she loves you?" James' expression was so pained, Roark had to turn his back.

"I don't know. We didn't discuss it. There wasn't time. We were in the shower and I felt her all around me and inside me like an explosion. It wasn't like the times before when we came together. It was more powerful, all-consuming. It left me weak and slow to react. Then, she started changing, shifting into one of them. Suddenly, her cousin was there in my bathroom, then her father, and—"

"Ugh, a family affair it seems," James said.

Roark arched a brow.

"Sorry, bad joke."

"I couldn't think and then suddenly, he's asking me if I mated her to me."

"Did you?"

"No. I wanted to. Truthfully, I've wanted to since the first moment I saw her standing at my front door. She doesn't have to say anything and I already feel as if I know everything about her. But I resisted. I didn't bite her. I always said I'd never mate to a woman without her permission. It just doesn't seem right."

"I agree. Besides, you have to get an elder's permission for it to be binding."

"Then Natasha said something about it being all her. That I didn't do it." Roark growled in frustration, running his hands through his long hair and pulling at it before letting go.

"This is touching to watch, but I haven't time to wait all day for you to figure it out, lycan."

Roark turned toward the bed and snarled, recognizing the voice as her cousin Dem. The farfadet looked almost human but for his light blue eyes, an impossibly clear shade for a mortal, and the light sparkling of navy blue skin on the sides of his eyes. Long blond hair hung from a ponytail on the top of his head, some of the strands crimped and others braided. His long silver tunic looked straight out of the Middle Ages, with a fantasy movie twist.

"What did you do with her?" Roark demanded, lurching forward.

Dem laughed, disappearing before Roark ever touched him. He reappeared next to James, winking audaciously at the man before disappearing again. Roark held still, breathing hard as his gaze darted around the room.

"Quite finished?" Dem asked.

"Where is she?" Roark demanded.

"I never thought my little cousin would go for one such as yourself. Lycans are very... What's the word? Neanderthal?" Dem smiled.

"You're one to talk, Twinkle Toes," James mumbled.

"Be nice," Dem ordered James. "Or I won't tell you what will happen to my cousin now that her new husband has rejected her."

"Husband?" Roark demanded, stepping between the two. Looking at Dem, he held up his hand, gesturing him to take it easy. "She really made me her husband?"

"Lot of good it did her. Sure, she got her powers back, only to be sacrificed because of your rejection."

"Sacrificed?" Roark and James said it at the same time. Feeling as if he'd been stabbed in the heart, Roark whispered, "She's dead?"

"What? I said, only to be sacrificed, didn't I? So sorry, old chap, I meant *set* to be sacrificed. Tomorrow. At dawn to be precise. Very poetic, isn't it? Sacrifices at dawn? There's a certain archaic quality to it. Ah, but what can you do?" Dem glided forward within a blink and patted Roark's shoulders. "Her parents are of the old ways. They believe mating is forever and if they can't be with their mate, then it's better to be dead. Not too many hard-core magics out there anymore, are there? Nope, they're a dying breed all right. Huh, kind of like my cousin."

It took all of Roark's control not to pummel the annoying man, though he did want to. "Where is she?"

His voice was hoarse and he shook violently. He vaguely heard James telling him through their telepathic link that farfadets were known for causing mischief.

"The question you should ask is, where will she be at dawn?"

"Come on, Roark, let's go find the lycan elders. They'll be more help to you than this fairy." James reached to a nearby box, grabbing out a shirt only to toss it at his naked brother.

"Whoa, wait," Dem said in a rush before quickly finding his arrogant nonchalance once more. "You said you loved her. Well, if that is true, then she'll be here," Dem swiped his hand through the air, showing an image of a rocky coastline.

"Where is that? Scotland?" James frowned.

"Aye," Dem said, affecting a Scottish accent. "'Tis."

"It could be a trick," James warned.

"There is no way I can get to Scotland before dawn, let alone find that coast. Even if we are mated, as you say, and I can sense her as my mate, the odds of me making it from Kansas to those cliffs are impossible."

"Ah." Dem closed his hand and the rocky cliffs disappeared. "That's where I come in." He reached into his tunic and pulled out a vial of dark red liquid.

"Blood?"

"Magic," he said.

Roark took it, uncorked the lid and sniffed. "It's blood."

"No, it is Natasha's blood and her magic," Dem corrected. "The family has been saving it for such a day. If your heart is pure and if you truly love her, it has the power to take you to her at dawn."

"But, why not use it now? Get her before the sacrifice," James reasoned.

"Sorry, it doesn't work that way. When you arrive, you will have to save her." Dem studied them both.

"Whose dawn? Here or Scotland?" Roark asked, looking at his hand.

"Ah, good question. Both. Farfadets slip through time. We build our homes in frozen seconds. We—"

"We get the idea," James said wryly. "Natasha's magic will supposedly slip him through the years to meet her at the right time and place within history— wherever you've hidden her."

"Hmm." Dem gave Roark's brother a sharp look before turning back to him. "I warn you. It won't be easy. In fact, it's likely the creature they plan on sacrificing her to will end up killing you both."

"What creature?" Roark asked, though if Natasha was in trouble, he knew he'd fight anything to save her—or, as Dem suggested, die trying.

"A fierce creature born within the icy waters of the Norwegian Sea," Dem said, his voice lowering an octave. "Feared for centuries, these creatures have terrorized fisherman, pulling their boats under the waves. And, if you were to kill it, the body would die only to be instantly reborn."

"A kraken?" James frowned. "They don't exist. All supernaturals know that. Inhabitants of fishing villages used to see the bodies of the creatures wash up on shore and the fisherman's wives needed something to blame for the deaths of their husbands. It's just a giant squid."

"They hardly look like a squid," Dem snorted. "Historical misconception."

"Are you saying krakens are real and Natasha is being sacrificed to one by her own family, unless I drink this vial and stop the creature from attacking her?" Roark's gut was tight with worry. How could her family do this? How dare they come into his home, take Natasha without giving him time to set things straight with her, without giving her time to explain what and who she was and why she was in his home?

"How do we know we can trust you?" James asked. "Roark, you can't be considering this. He's probably lying."

"That's part of the challenge. You don't. You may drink the blood and die a horrific death, or you may be transported to Medieval Europe or you might be taken right to where and when I said you will be."

Dem smiled. "As I've said, my kind does have the power to slip through dimensions and time. If your heart is pure, you'll make the right decision."

Roark couldn't take it. He balled his fist around the vial and punched Dem. The farfadet was taken by surprise and flew back, disappearing before he hit the wall.

"I'm glad you did that," James said, finding a pair of blue jeans and tossing them at Roark. "Because I was about to."

Roark caught the jeans with one hand as he looked at the vial in the other.

"Let's go find our father. He's dealt with magic before. Do you have your computer hooked up?" James headed for the bedroom door. "We should be able to get him on webcam."

"Yeah, back office, end of the hall." Roark slid on his jeans, still holding the vial of Natasha's blood. Then, grabbing the T-shirt he'd dropped on the floor, he followed James. His brother was already logging on when he got there.

## 10

Natasha looked at her cousin and frowned. The big chair dwarfed her, as she sat before the fireplace. The old castle was her childhood home—a place stopped in time for all eternity. In human reality, it had belonged to a duke that had died centuries before the current time. In their reality, a place in which every mortal deed, every word, every action was kept, time was forever frozen as their magical home, never changing, already decorated and furnished. Occasionally, the elders would let time slip, carrying them forward and back to change the decoration, to change where the duke and his household stood within the home, like statues. Maybe that's why farfadets weren't shy about sex. Natasha could remember several times as a young girl, almost a century ago, when she'd stumble into a room she used as her own, only to see mortal lovers frozen in a sexual embrace.

That was how all farfadets lived. They stole brief times in history and moved about as if they had forever. Living amongst mortals, but completely unseen, as they were frozen within a single second in the lives of mortals. Occasionally, there would be a strange flicker seen by human eyes as the two species passed, but it went by so fast the mortals never realized them for what they were—farfadets living amongst them in another state of existence. Farfadets traveled through time, moved through history like walking across a room, by the sheer desire to do so. It kept them hidden from other supernatural races as well as the mortals, their true defense of the ages. Strangely, there was a point where history ended, a sudden point that hadn't been lived yet in which the farfadet could not pass. If they tried, they'd stop, like hitting a brick wall they couldn't see or move past. Right now, that time was with Roark, technically the future of where she was now.

"Do you think he'll come for me, Dem?" she asked softly, turning to her cousin. He was older than her, but only by twenty years. She knew the elders thought them young and impulsive, even now. Her kind was immortal for the most part, unless—like in her, situation—the elders cursed them. Her curse had been mortality, but what had been a punishment had taught her a great amount about life.

Dem gave her a small smile, one that was most likely meant to be reassuring. He was nursing a black eye, one that Roark had given him. She knew he'd given her lover the vial of her blood laced with her magic and that Roark would have to truly feel something for her—regardless if he said it with words—in order to feel its power and come for her.

"Did he look like he would come?" she insisted.

"Nat, you know I can't tell you that," Dem answered. "Ask me again and the elders will most likely tell me I can't wait with you any longer."

Natasha nodded, knowing it to be true. Rubbing her temples, she felt the smooth skin by her eyes indicating her farfadet appearance. It was odd after all the years of looking human. But the full force of her transformational shift was over and she looked somewhat like her old self—the self Roark now knew her as. "I know, Dem, I know. I just can't stand this long wait."

"Long?" Dem laughed softly. "You call one night long? You have been among the mortals too long, haven't you?"

"I have a good life there," she said. Dem would never understand that. They grew up together, in magic, swimming through time. It's how they appeared to move so fast. They could freeze time. Too bad they couldn't speed it up.

"A good life? As a mortal? Doing what, Nat?"

"I taught etiquette to rich people."

Dem gasped, looking shocked before laughing heartily. Soon, she was joining him with a small giggle of her own. It was a little funny.

"You?" Dem demanded. "Etiquette? It was all your mother could do to make you act proper. Your lack of manners and etiquette was what got you into trouble in the first..." He paled, not finishing. "Oh, Nat, I'm sorry."

"Don't be. We both know what happened. There is no reason to skirt around the issue, is there? I defied my parents and the elders, and I was punished for refusing to marry when it was my 'time'. But the truth was, Dem, it wasn't my time. Until I saw Roark, it wasn't my time. I did what I must and in retaliation my father did as he must. As a human I had to learn to blend in, so I studied etiquette. I also needed a job and the company I work for happened to be hiring."

"Ugh, I didn't even think of that!" Dem

exclaimed, shivering. "A job? You couldn't even materialize your own money? Poor girl!"

"It wasn't so bad," she admitted. "It filled the hours."

"Well, you are home, now," Dem said.

"Yes, home. But for how long?" She again looked at the fire, thinking of Roark. The odds that he would come were slim. They'd only known each other for an incredibly short period of time.

"And yet you knew, didn't you?" Dem whispered, standing. "You knew."

Natasha glanced up at him, trying to read his blank expression. Was Dem trying to tell her something? Or was he just trying to give her hope? Cheer her up?

"Dem...?" she began, moving to stand.

"Demovoi!" an elder yelled from the door. "Come."

She knew the man had heard him. Dem didn't look at her as he walked away, but she saw the corner of his mouth shift into a subtle smile.

When she was alone, she took a deep breath.

*Roark, please, I beg you come for me. Please come. Don't leave me. Please, don't leave me.*

A pain washed over her as she thought of being left alone, tied to the cliff at the mercy of the kraken.

## 11

ROARK WAITED ALL NIGHT, staring at the clock on his living room wall as the hours ticked by. His father couldn't be of help and James had offered to stay and was sleeping in the guest bedroom.

Looking at his hand, to the vial he had yet to set down since it was given to him, he wasn't scared of facing death. He wasn't frightened by his own end. What did scare him was Natasha's death, of losing her, of having to live with the knowledge that he'd failed her.

Should he go ahead and drink the vial?

Did he have a choice?

Looking at the clock, he watched the minutes click by. Her cousin wouldn't want her dead, would he? Dem was her family. That had to count for something. The vial tingled in his hand and he opened it. Warmth spread over him and he smelled Natasha. Without bothering to wake his brother, he drank the blood.

"Roark?" James' voice penetrated his thoughts, but it was too late. His vision blurred, darkening as he felt a pull along his body. His back hit a wall and then another as he was pulled magically from the house. Scenery passed by, speeding faster and faster as he flew through the air. Minutes later he was dropped on the ground. Dawn peeked over the horizon and the sound of waves crashing on stone pierced his senses.

He was nauseated from his trip over the distance, but his fear for Natasha took over his body. Instantly, he shifted, instinctively knowing that would be the best way to find her. His bones cracked as fur grew over his body. He fell on all fours, his flesh rippling with the change.

Sniffing before his nose had fully turned, he caught her scent. Without thought of the danger, he ran for her. He had to get to her. If she was harmed, if they sacrificed her, he'd never forgive himself. He should've just said he claimed her. When her father asked, he should've grabbed her and refused to let go.

*Natasha,* he called out to her. *A thaisce...*

Suddenly, a scream rang out. She was by the cliffs. Without looking, he leapt over the edge of the earth toward the ocean. Roark howled as he fell through the air, bouncing his paws off the rocky incline as he fell, propelling his body toward her.

Natasha was tied to a wall of rock. Her magical appearance had faded, changing back into the human form she'd worn during her curse. Her red hair was pulled high on her head into a ponytail, crimped and braided in the farfadet style. Her blue eyes were turned toward the sea.

Natasha screamed again, her eyes widening. Roark landed on the ground. And that was when he saw it, the creature that caused her great fear. The kracken was a strange cross between an octopus and crab with sharp pinchers and tentacles for legs. Its head was more like a dragon with sharp fangs and big oval eyes. A black, inky substance clouded the water around it as the enormous sea monster pulled itself forward. Loud pops sounded as its suckers attacked themselves to the rocks along the shoreline. Roark's stomach tightened as he stood before Natasha, putting himself between the beast and her body.

"Roark!" Natasha gasped. "You came!"

Of course he came for her. How could he not?

❖

"Roark!" Natasha screamed, never so happy to see someone in her life. Her heart pounded in fear, but part of her had known he would come. Deep down, she knew her feelings had to be returned. But, just as she was happy to see him, to know he loved her, she was scared for him. "Roark, you have to get out of here! Save yourself, please."

He growled, his body partly shifting back to his human form as he stood on two legs. Hair still covered his body and fangs still glinted in his mouth. He rushed for her, reaching to grab the chains. The fearsome kraken growled behind him, roaring so hard that the wind shifted and blew against them.

"I'm not leaving you," he said, his voice gruff and hard. "I love you. I shouldn't have hesitated, but I promise you I will never falter again."

She opened her mouth to speak, but he surprised her by leaning forward toward her neck. Sharp fangs pieced her skin as he bit her. When he pulled back, blood dripped from his mouth.

"Roark?" she gasped, shaking.

"You are my wife, both in your way and mine. Not even death can stop what we have. If you are to die today, then so shall I. From this day forward, your fate is mine. Your life is mine and mine is yours. I love you, Natasha. The first moment I saw you I felt it. I'm sorry it took me so long to say it."

"But it was only a day," she whispered. The kraken growled again, but love replaced her fear.

"And after an eternity of living, it should not have taken me that long to know what I know now. I love you."

"Say it again," she whispered, grinning in the face of death. How could she feel anything but love when he was looking at her like that?

"I love you," he answered, shielding her with his body.

"And I you. I love you. I love you." She reached forward with her face, searching for his kiss. He kissed her. The kraken growled, sounding closer. The wind hit against them hard. Roark turned, ready to fight.

Natasha gasped. The great beast was gone and in its place stood her father, roaring like the creature.

"Father?" she asked, stunned to see him.

"It's about time, Button," he chuckled. "Damn youths. You're always so stubborn. Not like when I met your mother. We didn't have to have our lives threatened to admit when we were in love. Though we did have to get, ah, 'cursed' and sent away.

Though we were put into training camp for troubled farfadets. The humans were in some kind of war and I guess it inspired the idea with the elders."

"You were sent away?" Natasha gasped.

"Oh, you didn't really think you were a cursed mortal, did you? Like we could ever leave you like that." Her father laughed. "Everyone gets sent on a pilgrimage when it's their time. The longest one on record is fifty years, but Elder Angus was cursed to be an elf. That is when we started moving to mortals. The threat of a short life usually helps facilitate the process. Funny though, how you were sent to find a mortal—one we were completely prepared to magically change—only to come back with a lycan."

She stared at her father as she tried to process what was being said. This was all a test? She wasn't in trouble? There was no curse? She had never really been human? No wonder she'd felt parts of her magic rising up when she first met Roark, her mate. They'd only suppressed her powers, not taken them away.

"So there is no threat?" Roark said, shielding her. He was breathing hard, clearly not ready to let down his guard.

"No, no threat," the farfadet answered, smiling. "Welcome to the family."

"Ah, Father?" Natasha shook her chains. "Do you mind?"

"Oh, certainly." The farfadet nodded and the chains around her wrists melted away. She fell against Roark. Her body was weak from her fearful night and now the sudden relief.

"What?" Roark asked, still blocking her from a harm that was no longer there.

"You came through, dear boy." Her father laughed and glanced down at Roark's naked, shifted body. "When you two are done sorting things out, come back to the castle. Your family is waiting for you up there, my son, and I'm not sure the one called James believes that we meant no harm. Button, you know the frozen second in time in which we are living."

Natasha nodded, clinging to her husband. "Yes, I can find the time."

"Natasha?" Roark asked, pulling her close as her father disappeared.

"Time," she explained. "We live in seconds of time. So you have to not only know the place, but the second as well to find us."

He held her tighter. "I was so scared I'd lost you."

"I'm sorry about all this. We farfadets can be a little dramatic."

"Oh, baby, I'm so glad you're all right. When I heard that creature coming for you and felt your fear—"

"Shhh," she hushed him. "It's okay now. I didn't know, but I should've. My father wouldn't have let any harm come to me. I should've realized. But it's okay now. You're here. Now, let's go get your father's permission."

"For what?" he asked, leaning forward to kiss where he'd bitten her. His lips felt good and she shivered with longing. It had only been one night and yet she had missed his touch, needed it desperately.

"To get an elder's permission to marry so it's complete." She moaned accepting his touch without question or hesitation. It was like they'd known for an eternity, their souls just gliding through time until the day they met.

"I already did," he confessed, not pulling away as he began stroking her body. He pressed her up against the cliff. "Last night over webcam. It is official. You are my wife."

"Forever," she whispered.

"Yes, *a thaisce*," he said, kissing her deeply as if he would never let go. "Forever."

## THE END

THE SERIES CONTINUES...

## Call of Temptation
*Call of the Lycan Book 3*

James O'Connell lives simply, except for the whole hunting werewolves part. As one of the three lycan princes of the O'Connell clan, it's his duty to enforce the lycan law. When a member of their clan begins killing humans, he's sent to bring the rogue wolf in.

Claudia Hughes lives an ordinary life as a computer software analyst. Her mother and grandmother had psychic intuition, but hers is severely underdeveloped. Taking a solitary vacation, she trusted where instinct led her and ended up at the end of some crazy woman's fangs. She's led into a surreal world where lycans exist and passion for the man who saved her is the least of her worries.

🐾

## Excerpt

"Where is that bitch?" James O'Connell frowned, narrowing his eyes as he scanned the long balcony overlooking the sea. He breathed hard, sniffing the air as the full moon threatened him with a shift. Being a natural-born lycanthrope, he was ruled by the full moon but not controlled by it. More than that, he was called to the sea, for the moon controlled the tides just as it controlled the stirring of his blood. The sensation of power was like a drug and it caused many of his kind to live by the water.

His senses enhanced by the nature around him, he scanned the shadows along the wooden deck. A crisp breeze came off the Atlantic Ocean, stinging his nose as he tried to pick up on Meghan's elusive scent. Under his breath, he swore in frustration, "Fuck!"

He couldn't have lost her again, not after finally tracking her down on the somewhat remote island twelve miles off Rhode Island's mainland. Luckily for him, Meghan wasn't exactly the "camping-out" type and he didn't have to search the seventeen miles of shoreline to find her. All he had to do was go to the fanciest hotels and resorts on the island until someone recognized her photograph. It didn't take long. With Meghan's jet-black hair, tanned skin, generous breasts and penchant for wearing revealing clothing, she stood out in a crowd of humans like a walking goddess. Too bad this goddess was deadly.

Thinking to catch the barest hint of her scent, he began jogging along the deck. The beast lurking within him was fierce and always ready to unleash itself, but it was worse on the full moon, it was worse when it came to hunting Meghan. The bitch had nearly killed his oldest brother, Ian, future king of the O'Connell clan, and Ian's sea-swept bride, Ceana.

Technically, Ian was next in line to rule upon the death of the lycan king, their father, then James and finally the youngest, Roark. But, since they were immortal, unless some horrific event occurred, it was unlikely that any of the brothers would ever rule. James was fine with that. He would much rather have his family than a crown.

Roark, like James, had his own duties to the lycan clan. They were hunters, bringing justice to the rogue wolves—like Meghan—who broke their laws, meager laws that they were. She had betrayed the clan and tried to kill Ian when the oldest O'Connell didn't choose her as his bride and future queen. Though Ian and Meghan had a century-long affair of the flesh, James was very glad to know Ian hadn't tricked himself into thinking he loved Meghan. The bitch would no doubt have plotted to kill the king if she'd been next in line for the throne.

Meghan's crimes didn't end with her betrayal. After the assassination attempt, she had laid low for a while, ending up in Las Vegas where James was first able to track her down. Only after getting there did he realize she'd been a busy little lycan. She'd been killing showgirls and leaving their mutilated corpses in dark alleyways, as if taunting him with her misdeeds. When James got near and stopped her game, she'd been livid. Meghan had gone on a killing rampage, leaving a trail of human female corpses across Nevada, Idaho, Oregon and Washington. Some in the clan believed she'd gone up to Canada, but in truth, she'd merely tried to throw them off her scent, becoming more discreet about hiding her victims' bodies, as she turned her attention south, zigzagging a haphazard pattern across the United States.

Feasting on mortals was forbidden. It was one of the oldest of their laws. Lycans were an ancient people, their race as old as the humans', growing with the humans from a time when mortals knew of all the supernatural races. They used to be hunted, condemned as evil by the church. Sure, times were wilder in the early days, but so it was with all the races—mortal and supernatural. Just as humans no longer roamed the countryside pillaging and wielding swords so did his people no longer uncontrollably wield claw and fang.

In present times, humans denied their existence, which suited most of the supernaturals just fine. But their denial led them in circles when it came to Meghan, searching for a killer who could not be caught by their mortal means. With Roark newly married, it was up to James to find Meghan and punish her. It was a task that weighed heavily upon him, as she was proving to be a cunning adversary. And with each new victim, she seemed to grow stronger and more elusive.

Lucky for all, her killings had yet to result in a human being turned. Death came much easier to mortals than a changing. Not only would it be an embarrassment for the clan, since James was expected to prevent such a thing, it would be another burden James did not need—taking care of a young one. Circumstances had to be right, the bloodline perfect and the moon full for the bite to take effect. It fell into natural order that if attacking humans was against the law, so was trying to turn them. A lycan could attack fifty mortals and possibly only one would start to turn. Reason dictated that if one was turned, the odds were that many had been attacked. Even then it didn't guarantee the mortal would make it through the horrifically painful process.

"Fucking cunt!" James leapt over the stairs leading down to the sandy beach. The slippery footing didn't halt his progress as he sprinted along the shore. Stars spread out, punctuating the cloudless sky. Despite the cold sea air, that really didn't bother him, it was a perfect night. He would have preferred rain, as the foul weather would surely keep humans indoors. Though the beach appeared abandoned where he was, he could detect human voices in the distance. It prevented him from shifting and catching Meghan all the faster.

"No," a breathy whisper caught his attention. He started to ignore it as he filtered through the voices to find Meghan, but something in the way the word trembled kept his attention. "Get off me!"

James focused his thoughts, not breaking stride. The sounds of a struggle ensued, the unmistakable sounds of a fight. Light grunts pitted against an evil laugh. He'd been around too long not to recognize what happened. A mortal woman was caught in Meghan's grasp and, by the sound of it, she was putting up one hell of a fight. Amazement filled him at the mortal's stamina. Not many could stand up to a lycan, especially when being attacked.

"Ouch!" Meghan's voice swore. A loud smack followed the word. "You stupid, fucking cunt, you broke my rib! Oh, that's it. Playtime is over, you mortal piece of shit."

*Meghan!* James yelled, directing his thoughts toward the lycan woman. He used the telepathic link lycans shared to yell at her. *Stop!*

"Stay back." The woman's yell sounded closer than before, but it was still a long run down the beach. It was only by focusing his lycan hearing that he managed to catch the words. James shivered at the soft quality to her voice, even as she yelled at her attacker. The blood pumping in his veins made it easy for his cock to stir at the sound. "I don't know what you want or who you think you are, lady, but I don't want to have to hurt you."

"You, hurt me?" Meghan laughed harder.

"I will if I have to. I know how to defend myself. Just walk away," Meghan's victim answered.

Again James was amazed that the woman stood

up to a lycan. He could detect Meghan's anger by the way her loud breath pierced the night. Mortals would not be able to detect the sound but he could with his enhanced hearing.

*You have a choice, James. Save the girl or catch the queen.* Meghan's voice whispered through his thoughts. *I admit, I wonder which you will try to do.*

## To find out more about Michelle's books visit www.MichellePillow.com

# ABOUT MICHELLE M. PILLOW

## *New York Times* & *USA TODAY* Bestselling Author

Michelle loves to travel and try new things, whether it's a paranormal investigation of an old Vaudeville Theatre or climbing Mayan temples in Belize. She believes life is an adventure fueled by copious amounts of coffee.

Newly relocated to the American South, Michelle is involved in various film and documentary projects with her talented director husband. She is mom to a fantastic artist. And she's managed by a dog and cat who make sure she's meeting her deadlines.

For the most part she can be found wearing pajama pants and working in her office. There may or may not be dancing. It's all part of the creative process.

**Come say hello! Michelle loves talking with readers on social media!**

www.MichellePillow.com

facebook.com/AuthorMichellePillow

twitter.com/michellepillow

instagram.com/michellempillow

bookbub.com/authors/michelle-m-pillow

goodreads.com/Michelle_Pillow

amazon.com/author/michellepillow

youtube.com/michellepillow

pinterest.com/michellepillow

# COMPLIMENTARY EXCERPTS

## TRY BEFORE YOU BUY!

# THE DRAGON'S QUEEN

## BY MICHELLE M. PILLOW

Dragon Lords Series

*Bestselling Shape-shifter Romance*

Mede of the Draig knows three things for a fact: As the only female dragon-shifter of her people, she is special. She can kick the backside of any man. And she absolutely doesn't want to marry.

Mede has spent a lifetime trying to prove herself as strong as any male warrior. Unfortunately, being the special, rare creature she is, she's been claimed as the future bride to nearly three dozen Draig—each one confident that when they come for her hand in marriage fate will choose them. When the men aren't bragging about how they're going to marry her, they're acting like she's a delicate rare flower in need of their protection.

She is far from a shrinking solarflower.

Prince Llyr of the Draig knows four things for a fact: He is the future king of the dragon-shifters. He must act honorably in all ways. He absolutely, positively is meant to marry Lady Mede. And she dead set against marriage.

Llyr's fate rests in the hands of a woman determined not to have any man. With a new threat emerging amongst their cat shifting neighbors, a threat whose eyes are focused firmly on Mede, time may be running out. It is up to him to convince her to be his dragon queen.

❧

## The Dragon's Queen Excerpt

There were three things Medellyn knew for a fact. She was special. She could kick the ass of any boy. And she did not want to marry and have babies.

She was special.

Medellyn was one of the only dragon shifting females in all the universe, and definitely in all of the

Draig. Only once in a thousand births was a female dragon-shifter born. She was rare, or so everyone kept telling her. Her childhood was a strange contradiction. Her very proper mother tried to treat her as if she were some sacred crystal that might crack. Her warrior father tried to make her train like a boy while dressing like a girl.

She could kick the ass of any boy.

Medellyn hated when boys tried to act as if she were weak and to be protected. Her dragon was just as fierce as any of theirs, probably more so. To prove her point, she'd gladly pummel any who had challenged her to the ground...and some who hadn't.

She *absolutely, positively* did not want to marry and have babies.

Being the special, rare creature she was, in the twenty not-so-sweet girlhood years of her life she'd been claimed as the future bride to nearly three dozen boys—each one confident that when they came of the age to marry she would make their crystals glow and they hers.

Glowing crystals wasn't just a metaphor. On the day she was born, her father journeyed to Crystal Lake like all the new fathers did. He dove beneath the waves, swam down to the deepest part and pulled her stone from the lakebed. Like all Draig children, she wore the stone around her neck, and would continue to wear it until the day it glowed telling her which of the dragon shifting men she was destined by the gods to marry. Okay, technically she might be destined to marry an offworlder like most Draig men, but no one on her planet seemed to think so.

Gods bones, she hoped she wasn't destined to end up with any of the idiots on her planet. They had yet to impress her.

When it was her turn to go to the Breeding Festival, the crystal would glow signifying her *curse* for all to see. Well, her "blessing" as her mother called it. Lady Grace did not appreciate her daughter calling marriage a curse. Grace did not appreciate a lot of things that Medellyn liked, such as swords and bows, ceffyl riding, camping alone in the forest, hunting, sparring, smashing arrogant looks off of dragon men's faces.

It was a fight with her mother that sent her running through the mountain forest. Medellyn hated the woman, hated what her mother wanted her daughter to be. Grace was only a human, brought to their planet as a bartered bride. She married Medellyn's father without question and spent most of her days completely in docile agreement with whatever her husband said. Medellyn couldn't imagine taking anyone else's opinions over her own.

Her father, Axell, was a highly praised warrior in the Draig army and carried the title of Top Breeder of the ceffyls. The man's whole life focused on four things: his wife, his only child, and mares and steeds. Her father was a very important man, but his work kept him away from home several nights a week as he slept outdoors with the herd. With a three-year gestation period and only about fifty percent live-birth rate, the animals were not a resource that could be easily renewed. His ceffyls supplied the soldiers with mounts and farmers used them for beasts of burden to help with the fields.

Like Axell, Medellyn was a proud dragon. Had she been born male, she would have been a warrior, too. Instead, she was *special*. How could her human mother begin to understand the wildness than ran in her dragon blood? If she had, Grace would never have asked Medellyn to tame her spirit.

Breathing hard, she came to an abrupt halt and screamed into the trees. Her body shook with rage and she tore at the pretty gown she wore. She hated her body, hated being special, hated being expected to act like a lady when she felt like a dragon. Her taloned finger snagged on the crystal around her neck and she cut the leather strap of the necklace. The crystal flew several feet away.

"I am not some man's chattel," she yelled, knowing she'd run far enough away that her mother could not hear her retorts. Since she was shifted her voice was hoarse and powerful, and she reveled in the fierceness of it. "I am not some breeding ceffyl to have children. It is not my place to give you fifty grandkids. I can't help you only had one child. If you would have made me a boy, I wouldn't be a disappointment to you!"

Tears stung her eyes as Medellyn walked aimlessly, searching the forest floor for the fallen necklace. Finding it, she grabbed the inert crystal into her fist. It was a reminder of all she was expected to be. She took a deep breath, looking at her fist and then to the stones littering the forest floor. A small smile formed on her mouth. Medellyn dropped the crystal on the hard ground and glared at it. Rage boiled inside her, the kind of rage surely only a dragon-shifter could feel.

"This is what I think of your fate," she growled as she fell to her knees.

Medellyn grabbed a heavy rock and smashed it down onto her necklace. The crystal cracked. The noise gave her some satisfaction so she hit it again.

Grunting with each strike of the stone, she didn't stop until her future had been ground to dust.

"That is what I think of your destiny."

**To find out more about Michelle's books
visit www.MichellePillow.com**

# PERFECT PRINCE

## BY MICHELLE M. PILLOW

Dragon Lords Series

*A Perfect Escape...*

Nadja Aleksander has everything she could ever want in life, except her freedom. Skipping out on her engagement, to a man her controlling father has chosen for her, Nadja books passage on the first spaceship she can find. Bound for a planet of primitive humanoid males, Nadja plans on finding a simple, hardworking man who will allow her to live out her days in total obscurity.

*A Perfect Mistake...*

Dragon-shifter Prince Olek is pleased with his refined and blushing bride. When she chooses him to be her life mate, appearing happy in her decision, his heart soars—until the next morning when his new princess wants nothing to do with him. Olek doesn't know what he's done to upset his alluring bride, but he is determined to reignite the hot sparks that burned the night they met.

❧

## Perfect Prince Excerpt

"Come, bride."

Again, she couldn't deny him, moving to dip under the green tent flap he held up for her. When she drew near him, she smelled the warm oil on his glistening skin. It mixed with the natural scent of him. She breathed deeply. This was as close as she had ever been to such an inadequately dressed man before.

She faltered in her movements, glancing up into his eyes. Before she knew what was happening, a strong hand was on her face, gently cupping her cheek. The touch was fire to her already flushed features. Her lips parted with a ragged, scared gasp. Olek took it as an invitation and dipped his head forward.

Nadja almost screamed when he tried to kiss her. Her first reaction was to run. Dodging under his arm, she darted inside the tent. Nadja froze mid-step as she looked around. The red earth floor was covered completely in soft furs. It cushioned her feet beneath her slippers. Below the center point of the pyramid was a high platform bed, which required a step to climb onto it. Silk hung down around the sides, stirring delicately in the torchlight like soft white clouds.

She should have run *out* of the tent, not in.

Spinning to do just that, she realized the only exit was still blocked. She was trapped. Olek grinned, though the look seemed baffled.

"I-I," she stuttered, not sure how to explain her rude behavior, or if she even should.

Olek let the flap fall shut behind him as he followed her inside. He resembled a stalking beast after his prey, relishing the anticipation of the hunt.

Nadja turned from him and was again met with the giant bed. She recoiled from it as if it was covered in poison. It occurred to her how intimate this night really could be. Stumbling back, she bumped into an incredibly hard chest.

She jolted in panic, scurrying away from the solid, warm muscles. Her eyes darted around, taking in the three corners of the enclosure. In the first, there was a bath drawn, the steaming water coming out of the basin. A sweet perfumed scent rose with it. Folded towels, bath oils, and rinses were neatly arranged at the side.

The next corner had a table full of chocolates, fruits and cream sauces. A bench with cushioned seats stretched along the side, resembling a couch. An earthen wine jug was set in the center. Feeling the heady consequences of the liquor she had drunk too much of at the feast, she turned away from the food.

The third corner, behind the bed, was harder to see from her position so she ignored it. Feeling rather than hearing Olek coming up behind her, she again panicked. Swirling to face him, she held up her arms and backed away. Her hands shook. This was not how she imagined being alone with a man would feel like. She always assumed it would be like reporting to one of the robot guards, or talking to a dignitary at some function she was forced to attend.

But Olek was half naked and smiling at her like he knew every thought in her head. Did he somehow realize she liked looking at his oiled chest, to the point where she made a conscious effort not to? Could he know that when his hand had briefly held hers, her nerves had tingled, were still tingling? That the idea of his kisses both excited and terrified her?

Merriment poured from his gaze and she blushed to see it. He held back, standing tall as Nadja studied him. Before she realized it, her eyes were traveling a seductive journey of discovery over his taut chest. Already his small nipples were hard buds. His flesh dipped in all the right places only to rise and swell with each of his shallow breaths. There was no fat on his chiseled form and she doubted they employed beauty services to remove fat cells on a planet like this. His body was all natural. She bit her bottom lip, absently chewing at it as she looked him over.

His broad shoulders carried his strong arms with ease. They were arms that could crush her if he so chose. The metal band on his biceps would have fit on top of her head like a crown. Looking closer, she saw that the jewelry was shaped like a dragon winding over flesh.

Nadja looked at his covered face. He did indeed appear bold and strong like a dragon.

"Are you pleased?" he asked confidently when she didn't move. Again, his smile was alluring and light. She could tell by the expression that this was a man who laughed often.

She blinked nervously, trying to erase the image

of tight flesh burning into her memory. He took a step forward, moving as if to touch her.

"No," she commanded, her eyes narrowing. Her words stopped him. Her breathing deepened. "Just stay back a moment."

His head tilted to the side, waiting for her command.

Nadja took another deep breath, trying to control her undisciplined emotions and wild heartbeat.

"I don't think there is a need to do any of..." She swallowed nervously and looked at the bath and then the bed. Shivering, she tried to lift her hands to cross protectively over her chest and grew frustrated by the binding straps. With a frown, she tugged the belt off her arms. "I meant to say, I know the tradition of this night is to prove yourself a worthy mate by a display of your..."

As Olek arched a brow, she saw the shifting beneath his mask. His eyes dipped to focus on the way her breasts bounced with her jerking movements. She freed herself from the arm ties and left them to hang at her waist.

Swallowing over her embarrassment, she crossed her arms over her chest to break his gaze, and uttered, "Your prowess."

The grin widened over his amazingly firm lips.

Those lips weren't fair. No man should look that delectable. Nadja made a small sound of distress before continuing. She knew he wanted her to choose him for her husband. It wasn't fair. He couldn't really speak until she granted him permission. The only way to grant him permission was to accept him as a husband. Hurting his feelings wasn't a great way to start off their possible life together, so she tried to speak carefully.

"I am telling you, there is no need for that. I am not concerned with..." Nadja felt like kicking herself. The words sounded weak and trembling. Normally she could speak with soft confidence, always reasonable and logical and well-phrased. Her voice came out in hot, breathless pants. What was he doing to her? Her body felt like it was on fire, like she needed to take off her clothes and jump into a snow drift. She started to sweat. Absently, she fanned her face, trying to concentrate. Forgetting where she had left off, she repeated, "I am not concerned with your prowess —*ah!*"

Olek boldly whipped his loincloth from his hips and dropped it to the fur-lined floor.

**To find out more about Michelle's books
visit www.MichellePillow.com**

PLEASE LEAVE A REVIEW

THANK YOU FOR READING!

Please take a moment to share your thoughts by reviewing this book.

Be sure to check out Michelle's other titles at www.MichellePillow.com